THE
SPACE
BETWEEN
TWO
DEATHS
W0006965
JAMIE
YOURDON

Supervising Editor: Caitlin Chrismon
Associate Editor: Aleshia Scogin
Cover Designer: L. Austen Johnson

ISBN (paperback): 978-1-952919-00-8

GenZPublishing.org
Aberdeen, NJ

For Beth. WAAR.

PROLOGUE

THE ARMY of Nippur attacked before dawn.

Scouts entered the city of Uruk through a half-dozen gates, followed soon thereafter by infantry soldiers who surged down the uneven streets. For many of the young men, it was their first military campaign, a fact reflected by their behavior. They sang songs, excoriated one another, and made horseplay.

Soldiers entered houses at random—one-story, mud-brick structures grouped around open courtyards, where dazed Urukians soon found themselves cornered, befuddled by sleep and armed only with cooking implements. They wept and panted—they reeked of terror. Men above the age of nine were slaughtered. Survivors would fetch a good price as slaves, even their now-defiled wives and daughters.

Meanwhile, the Nippurians stole gifts for their loved ones and made jokes to soothe their nerves.

By first light, the sky over Uruk was hazy with smoke. What little resistance the soldiers had encountered, they'd gleefully quashed. As they made their way toward the central ziggurat, with its unique vantage point and terraced steps, they expected to find the worshippers of Enlil waiting for them. It was common during the summer months for one Sumerian city-state to invade another and, in doing so, to raze their temples and kill their zagmi. On this day, however, the Nippurian soldiers would encounter something different.

Inside the ziggurat, their footsteps echoed. Immense statues of Enlil gazed down at them, with devotional jars of honey placed at his sandaled feet. Below the main shrine were rooms meant for food storage, as well as a mausoleum for the city's mitu, and it was here that the soldiers found the zagmi and their stewards. Not a single one was still alive.

They'd all ingested poison—a variety of berry that stained the tongue when chewed but was also fatal at a sufficient volume. It appeared that the worshippers of Enlil, privy to their fate, had embraced death on their own terms. In room after room, the soldiers encountered their corpses, bellies distended and tongues blackened, bowels emptied upon the floor, each face a hideous mask. For every zagmi, they counted four stewards, boys with shaved heads and eyebrows, some only recently parted from their mothers, often clinging to each other in death. Perhaps the soldiers thought of their own siblings back home or the succor of childhood they'd so recently enjoyed. Each level yielded more rooms and more bodies, their skin still warm. The silence deepened.

The soldiers were distraught. They tore at their hair and swallowed their tears. This was not the natural order of things. It was their prerogative to kill the zagmi, not the zagmi's prerogative to kill themselves. As word of the mass suicide spread among the ranks, a greater concern surfaced, one that could be seen on every face. If the zagmi could orchestrate their own death, what further authority was forfeit? What power had the Nippurians ultimately ceded?

On this day, the army of Nippur killed everything. Every woman or child who'd been spared for auction. Every household pet or stray animal. The soldiers became the gears of a terrible machine. They were rage and savagery. Even some of the soldiers who'd been present at the temple were murdered by their peers simply for bearing witness.

Gone was their laughter from before. There was no joy taken in this reprisal. Once every dwelling had been searched and the final death toll had been tallied, the city of Uruk was incinerated to affirm the dominance of Nippur.

There would be another consequence.

For the first time in recorded history, more mitu now populated the netherworld than living souls populated the natural world. The wholesale death of so many men, women, and children had tipped the scales. As a result of this imbalance, a rift occurred. The netherworld swelled to accommodate its growing ranks and to represent its newfound prominence, thus testing the boundaries of the natural world. The earth split in two.

This phenomenon could be observed for miles around, far beyond the ashes of Uruk, where people of many nations would comment on the disturbance, speculate, and then resume their normal lives.

1

ZIZ

As soon as Ziz had completed a task assigned by her mother, there would always be another task, and then another, until she'd been working from dawn until dusk with no time left for play. To be the child of a farmer meant to be a farmer oneself. There was no respite unless she claimed it—and so, on this particular afternoon, Ziz was hiding in the vegetable garden in the shade of a date palm, narrating a story. She knew if she hid long enough, her mother, Meshara, would become preoccupied and lose track of her. This was easier to accomplish when her father, Temen, was absent from the farm, just as he was on this day.

Amid the rows of lentils and chickpeas, Ziz commanded a view of the animal pens, where the pigs stood listlessly and chickens dithered in the dirt.

She was supposed to be picking mustard seeds. This was the chore that Meshara had assigned, as tedious as it was insignificant, by Ziz's reckoning. If her mother were to appear by her side, Ziz could point to her clay bowl and pile of seeds and complain about the day's heat. But Meshara was engaged with a task, too, clearing irrigation canals on the other side of the wheat field. She was unlikely to return to the family dwelling before the evening meal.

"In the time before time," Ziz began, "the god An asked the goddess Ninhursag to be his bride. He said, 'I love you—will you marry me?' But the goddess said no. 'Why not,' he said? 'Because,' she replied, 'I am free! I belong to no one.'

"The god's feelings were hurt, but Ninhursag didn't care. She ate honey cakes all day and chased frogs by the Euphrates. After she fell asleep, An captured her anyway. 'Wake up,' he said! 'We're married!' And he dragged her by the hair to his home on the highest peak of Mashu."

To represent An, Ziz held a doll that Temen had made for her. The doll was in poor condition—its stone features had lost their detail and one of its feet was missing. In her other hand, she held a piece of cheesecloth meant to represent Ninhursag, bundled around an onion and cinched to form a head. Temen had promised to make her another doll, but there was never time. Now, Ziz suspected, she was too old for toys. Her parents demanded that she trade play for labor, a bargain that made her feel lonely and sometimes angry. No children lived close enough to compare her experience with, so she imagined her fate to be worse than that of others.

"The goddess was very sad," she continued, shifting to a kneeling position and tucking the folds of her dress under her shins. "Ninhursag didn't want to be An's wife or anyone else's, so she decided to fool the god. That night, while he slept, she cut off all her hair and yanked out all her teeth. In the morning, when he awoke, she said, 'Good morning, husband! Tell me your dreams.'"

Ziz was familiar with her parents' stories. Meshara liked to narrate as she cooked. Temen more often used stories to divine meaning, like the time Ziz had dreamed she'd eaten a wasp nest and he'd forbidden her from speaking for three days, slapping her when she laughed by accident. With this particular tale, each of her parents emphasized a different aspect—Temen, the confusion and disappointment of An, and Meshara, the cleverness of Ninhursag. Ziz shared her mother's sympathies. During the times when her body ached from her father's blows, Ziz thought of the goddess, her raw scalp and bloody gums, and tried to feel in possession of herself.

"An was surprised," Ziz said. In her deepest voice, she bellowed, "'Who are you? Where is my wife?' The goddess said, 'Don't you recognize me?' 'No,' An said. 'You're ugly!' So he forced her from his home, and Ninhursag returned to the Euphrates, where she decided not to grow her hair back or even her teeth. Instead, she remained that way, so no man would ever bother her again. Only when she looked at her reflection in the water could she see her true self."

For good measure, Ziz used doll-Ninhursag to give doll-An a whack before dropping him in the soil. "'Ugh,'" she groaned in An's voice. "'You win.'"

Ziz looked up. Perhaps something in her peripheral vision had alerted her, but she now saw Temen walking alongside the wheat field. Her father was tall, with bulbous joints connecting his too-long limbs. Unlike Ziz, who shared her mother's round face and abundant curly hair, Temen's profile was gaunt, his head and cheeks shaved. Indeed, the only attribute he and Ziz shared was their fair complexion, lighter than Meshara's, like nuts from a different tree. Temen stood at a distance, where he couldn't hear her. Nor, Ziz suspected, could he see her, given the plants around her and her low-lying position.

She was reluctant to rise.

Temen had traveled to Nippur to arrange a marriage. At the age of ten, Ziz was old enough to be betrothed, but not old enough to be a wife—Meshara had repeatedly assured her of this. She wouldn't become a woman for years to come, a rite of passage that involved bleeding and a man's unwillingness to address it, as well as the guidance and protection of the goddess Ninhursag. Ziz had been relieved beyond words. The likelihood of being paired with a man like her father filled her with dread.

However, it wasn't too early to find a prospective husband. Temen had planned his trip for early summer, when a military campaign against Uruk would rid the city of brawling young men. His journey had lasted many days, during which time Ziz had prayed for his delay, by brigands, flood, or disease. And now he was back.

Finally, her curiosity overtook her. After rocking back and forth on her heels more times than she could count, Ziz set aside her dolls and walked down the incline.

Ziz entertained the idea that different emotions spoke at different volumes, like competing voices in a crowd. What would be the loudest emotion, she wondered? Anger? Fear? Happy feelings would be quieter, obviously, but did that mean they were of lesser value? It was possible that she could feel many things at once but could only *hear* one emotion at a time. The question was a welcome distraction as she approached her father, the grass pliant beneath her feet.

"Hello, father," she greeted Temen when she was close enough to be heard.

He kept his eyes fixed on the ground. "Is your mother doing something different?"

The sound of his voice made her stomach clench. Ziz looked at the same patch of soil—otherwise unremarkable, between the shin-high rows of wheat.

"Something with the dirt," Temen qualified.

He turned to her for an answer. Inwardly, Ziz cringed the way she did whenever Temen directed his attention toward her. Outwardly, she shrugged. She was only vaguely curious about the farm's operation, its planting, irrigation, and harvesting cycles. It was Meshara who spent long hours in the sun, encouraging their crops to flourish. No wonder her skin was a darker color.

When it became clear that Ziz didn't possess any information, Temen grunted and looked down. Ziz felt the disappointment of her failure, but she ignored this emotion—another voice added to the choir—and chanced a question of her own.

"Do you have any news for me? From Nippur?"

"You will marry a soldier."

All at once, she experienced numerous sensations, dizziness and nausea being chief among them.

It was happening. However fast or slow, and despite what she might've wished for herself, Ziz would be made a bride. Briefly, she had the thought that she should've finished her chore, as if the collection of mustard seeds were related to her marriage prospects.

Temen studied her. "You're unhappy?"

"A soldier," Ziz echoed him, forcing herself to swallow. "Thank you, father."

"His family owns this farmland. His father was a soldier, too, when he was young—now they live in a house with many rooms. I suppose your sons will also grow up to be soldiers, if you're lucky."

"Thank you," she said again.

Ziz knew she shouldn't be surprised. The majority of Sumerian men would rather join the army than apprentice at a craft, such as carpentry or leatherwork. Yet her mind raced. What would her new husband look like? A bearded face, in all likelihood, if he were old enough to grow a beard, with long hair parted down the middle. But what about his eyes? Would they be kind? Would he have killed many men by the time that she met him?

"What?" Temen said. His hands remained at his sides, where Ziz watched them.

"It's just—" She stammered. "Must I marry him?"

Temen stared at her, incredulous. His right hand twitched.

"You're complaining?"

"No, I just—"

"Soldiers travel for half the year. They enjoy the gods' favor. They're always paid on time—not counting what they take for themselves—and most of them die young. His family will support you, so long as you bear his children. You are a farmer, Ziz. I am a farmer. Do you want your children to be farmers? *I* don't want to be—I want to be free of this place."

"How soon?" she asked him.

Temen reached into the folds of his dress. "The bridal gift must be paid," he said. "Normally, your husband would do it, but his father will make the trip instead. He'll be here in a few days' time. He gave me this."

Temen presented her with a stone cylinder. Ziz had never held one before, but she knew what it was —an engraving that would manifest an illustration when rolled over a clay tablet. She wondered why her potential husband couldn't make the trip himself and determined it was probably because he was engaged in bloodshed.

"They showed it to me," Temen said. "A battlefield scene with many warriors—"

"Mimma," Ziz interrupted. "How soon until I'm married?"

Her impertinence surprised them both, but Ziz couldn't help herself. She had to know. She watched Temen for a response, ready to absorb whatever punishment was due. Her father narrowed his eyes.

"I already told you. Once the bridal gift has been paid."

Not another year or two, then, but a matter of days. This was far sooner than Ziz had expected. Meshara had lied to her, a betrayal that Ziz had never experienced before. Maybe she'd be allowed to stay on the farm a while longer? Ziz thought of the mustard seeds sitting in the garden. Her parents would require her help for the harvest. She could be helpful—really, she could. To be made a wife before she was counted among women seemed grossly unfair. Squeezing the stone cylinder in her fist, she glared at her father, who showed no sign of sympathy.

"Your children—" he said again.

Then the ground ripped in two.

A terrible noise originated beneath their feet, accompanied by a shaking motion. Ziz pressed her palms to her ears, staggering away from the widening ravine where insects, grass root, and schist had already been exposed. Two tiers formed, one high and one low, with Ziz and Temen standing on the lower portion. In the distance, Ziz could hear livestock screaming and what must've been a date palm being wrenched from the earth. The same violence was wrought upon every living thing.

Had she angered An with her impertinence? Or was it Ninhursag, protecting her from an undesirable marriage? Even with her limited appreciation, Ziz knew the damage to the farm would be devastating —crops flooded, animals scattered and lost, not to mention losing whatever vanished into the earth, where it would become the property of the netherworld. Death above and death below.

As the tremors subsided, she could see Meshara running toward them. From a distance, her mother's eyes appeared wide, the smooth contours of her face pocked with concern. It was the face of a liar, Ziz thought to herself, a liar or a fool. Meshara had promised her. She'd *promised* there'd be more time. And now Ziz's future was all but assured.

Temen's mouth was also moving, but Ziz couldn't make out the words. Looking down, she remembered the stone cylinder in her hand. The image of her husband's face floated before her, this man who'd make her a woman too soon. Beard or no beard, he horrified her. Let her remain a child a while longer, Ziz thought. She turned and threw the cylinder into the ravine. The polished stone caught the light and winked at her before it also disappeared.

2

MESHARA

MESHARA LIVED IN SILT. It shifted in her sleep; it rode the eddy of her dreams. Upon waking, her head would feel heavy, so she'd occupy herself with other concerns. Enough time had passed to determine which crops had been lost, either to the ravine itself or because the irrigation system had flooded, drowning the fields she'd so recently planted. When her mental list grew exhaustive, she switched to an accounting of what still remained, mostly livestock and the contents of their root cellar. And each other, for what it was worth.

The family had gathered in the dwelling, a circular enclosure that contained their sleeping mats, cooking implements, and an unoccupied stool. Ziz was kneading dough for bread. Temen stood in the doorway, doubtlessly entertaining his strange notions about the ravine. One had only to look at him to see. On three separate occasions, he'd described the sound it made, like the gods were trying to get his attention. Perhaps if Meshara would be willing to join him there, his visits would've ceased. But why cater to him? The state of their farm should've been cause for alarm—even cause for panic, just as it was for her—a fuzziness on the edges of things.

"We need to drain the fields again," she said. Her statement was obvious, but it helped Meshara to think aloud. "The ground will dry faster than springtime," she added, "there's that advantage. But the weeds will grow faster, too, and the ox will be stubborn. Especially that old cow. Do you know the one I speak of? She doesn't like change. She dislikes it even when I tie my hair back."

This last comment had been meant as a joke, but Temen didn't respond. It was too hot for humor. Ostensibly, they'd retreated to the dwelling to avoid the midday heat, but the cookfire had rendered even this space uncomfortable.

Ziz was making her loaves too big. Meshara slapped her daughter on the back of the hand, harder than was necessary, to get her attention. Ziz winced.

"I'm nervous. We don't have enough seeds for a full harvest," Meshara said, tearing a patty in half to demonstrate the proper size. "We're lucky we have any. We could ask for help from a neighbor, but most of them will face the same problem. I think we should concentrate on barley. Temen? We've never drained the fields twice before—we've never had to. I'm worried the salt will make it harder to grow wheat. Barley is a sturdier crop, don't you think?"

"Hmm?" Temen murmured. "Yes, I suppose."

"Don't *suppose*." Meshara snapped at him. The words flew from her mouth before she knew it. "This is the food we eat—the food to keep us from starving. *Know* it's a good idea."

Temen glared at her from across the room. Yes, she had gained his attention, but she'd also provoked his ire. Was he insulted by the implication he couldn't feed his family? Or the deeper cut that he knew less about farming than she, the daughter of a basket weaver, who'd learned the trade from Temen's father? It galled him, Meshara knew, as well it should. It galled her, too.

She held his gaze for as long as she was able. Finally, she looked down.

"Barley," Temen agreed. "If we have the seeds, we'll plant barley."

"Are we really going to starve?" asked Ziz.

Meshara could've hit her again. Only now the thought occurred to her? And what was her response, other than to create disproportionate loaves of bread? At Ziz's age, Meshara had already been an expert basket weaver, a proficiency that had served her not at all upon marrying a farmer. With the birth of a daughter, she'd expected to gain an ally. Instead, Ziz reflected Temen's worst characteristics, laziness and indecision chief among them. Perhaps a different parent would've spared her the truth, but Meshara couldn't afford to be generous. She desperately needed help—help that no one seemed to be willing or able to give.

"Of course we have enough food," Temen said. "Your mother worries over nothing. There are vegetables from the garden and what I catch in my traps. We'll be fine. The ravine shouldn't be seen as something that happened to us. It's—"

"A message?" Ziz interrupted him.

There it was. The spark to his imagination. "Yes," he said, his eyes widening. "A message from the gods."

With this, Meshara could feel the silt moving. It seemed to gather in her sinuses, until she wanted to lay her cheek upon the ground. It made a noise, the silt—a hissing sound. She imagined it traveling the length of the irrigation canals, dredged up from the bottom of the Euphrates River, first on seasonal floods and now this recent disaster. It stymied the passage of water, causing natural dams in places where additional flooding would later occur. It would have to be cleared by hand. Patiently, laboriously.

Only when all the silt had been removed could there be any hope for survival—if they had enough seeds, if the fields were dry in time, if the crop wasn't poisoned by salt. Meshara was sick with worry, as if a morsel of food had lodged in her esophagus.

"Clearly, it was the gods' will," Temen said, still speaking of the ravine. Ziz watched him, rapt, neglecting her dough. "There's no other explanation."

"Hamta!" Meshara barked, too enraged to consider the ramifications. "No more of this, Temen —do you hear me? No more nonsense about the ravine. I won't have it. Not another word. We need a plan. You need to remember your responsibilities. If this farm dies, it dies because of you."

"Ziz," Temen said, though in truth, he spoke to Meshara. "Go outside."

Now the silt hissed like a snake.

"Yes," Meshara agreed, encouraging Ziz to her feet—the faster, the better. Soon enough, Ziz would have her own version of Temen to deal with, but Meshara could protect her from that reality for a while longer.

"Go and get onion, garlic, carrot, and lentils," she said. "I'll finish the bread. Be sure to pick out any rocks and stones. When you get back, we'll make stew."

Ziz didn't need to be told twice—she exited the

dwelling with her eyes downcast. She expressed neither sympathy nor chagrin, but a preternatural awareness of the moment. She wouldn't return until the sun was lower in the sky and Meshara's punishment had been meted out. The whole time his daughter was in motion, Temen watched Meshara, not sparing a word for his child.

Once Ziz had gone, Meshara crossed the distance between them. Although it was too late for words, she continued to reason with him. "Temen," she said. "We need a plan. We need to—"

He struck her with a closed fist. He didn't need to move. Meshara had brought herself within range, and now she collapsed on the floor. The blow was both expected and unexpected. Meshara waited for more—a kick, perhaps, or an item to be hurled at her. At the same time, she experienced a sickening wave of gratitude for this violence. It gave her a reason to hate him beyond his incompetence.

"I am your husband," Temen said, sounding not the least bit riled. "This is my farm."

From where she lay, Meshara considered the mounds of dough by the cookfire, each one uniquely ugly. She considered how he'd kneaded her body like she kneaded the bread, a funny idea, though she dared not smile. To laugh or cry would risk further wrath. Previously, Temen had struck her on the face, on her limbs, or on her back. There was no place he hadn't touched her in anger.

"Do you hear me?" he asked.

Meshara rose. "Yes."

"Garash is coming. He will be here tomorrow—possibly the next day."

Meshara opened and closed her mouth. Their landlord? Here? Had he heard about the rift? Was it Garash's intent to assess the farm? Were they in danger of losing it, more so than usual?

Why had Temen waited so long to share this information with Meshara, rather than telling her the moment he knew? She considered the possibility that he might be lying, but the details of his claim were too specific. Temen was watching her carefully, no doubt anticipating a slew of questions, and the look on his face…despite her anxiety, Meshara knew better than to goad him. There was still time to accrue knowledge—time to plan for Garash's arrival, no matter how imminent. First, though, they had to reconcile, a negotiation she well understood.

"Yes, husband," she said.

The day continued thereafter. Meshara's jaw ached. No doubt there would be a bruise, but no one commented on it. She and Ziz made stew, and later that night—after Ziz had retired to her sleeping mat and turned to face the fire—Meshara approached Temen. Just as before, he was standing in the doorway, staring into the night. Meshara spoke his name, imbuing her voice with all the tenderness she possessed.

"Temen."

She stood beside him, pressing one palm between his shoulder blades and the other to his chest, forming a vice between the two. She could feel his heart beating. Her own heart maintained a distant rhythm. Her life was bound to this man, Meshara reminded herself. She needed him and he needed her. If he'd forgotten this fact, it behooved her to remind him.

"Come," she said, leading him to their normal place on the floor. Meshara coaxed Temen to his knees and onto to his back. She could feel his reticence, his desire to occupy the doorway and, beyond that, to explore the ravine. It stung her pride, but she focused on her task.

When Meshara straddled him, she conveyed his hands to her waist, leaning forward until her nipples chafed against her dress. Temen stirred beneath her. She leaned even further, kissing one of his eyelids closed.

"Husband," she said. Unbidden, he moved a hand to her breast.

She kissed the other eyelid closed. "Husband," she said again, this time whispering in his ear. Using his free hand, he redistributed layers of fabric until nothing remained between them. Temen buffeted his groin against her thighs. Meshara wished to prolong the moment while they still remained separate, but in one fortuitous motion, he thrust his penis inside her. To accommodate this intrusion, she sat upright —her spine extended, her lungs full, her fingers trailing down his abdomen.

"Mine," she said. She delivered this syllable softly. Yes, she was addressing Temen, but also the gods, especially Ninhursag. Meshara imagined the word to be a tiny seed, blessed to grow to fruition.

Already he was engaged in fitful motions. Using her pelvis, she dictated a more gradual rhythm. In this way, they shared the effort. Temen's hands rested on her hips, occasionally returning to her breasts, where she endured his eager, if insistent, squeezing. Meshara couldn't see his eyes in the dark, only that they were open.

"Mine," she said again, her voice louder.

He was slowly becoming less pliable. When she could feel him nearing an end, Meshara reached between her legs. At her touch, the goddess thrilled through her body, suffusing every motion, every breath, with divine urgency. She encouraged Ninhursag with slow, circular motions until the pleasure became nearly unbearable. Soon thereafter, Temen bucked. Meshara occupied her own rapturous state for a moment longer, sitting astride her husband, before she lowered herself to the floor. The goddess abandoned the two lovers.

Temen's chest rose and fell. Ziz remained asleep—the sounds of her breathing and the hissing of the fire combining to fill the dwelling. Meshara stretched a leg over her husband. The presence of the goddess, which she could still identify in her joints and limbs, gave her strength. Meshara was in command again. If she could fully appreciate the situation, she could guide it to the desired conclusion. Nestled in the space between Temen's arm and ribcage, she gently spoke to him.

"Why is Garash coming?" she asked. "Did he tell you?"

It made no difference whether he withheld the answer or had truly fallen asleep. Temen didn't speak.

3

CROW

THE CROW STOOD AWKWARDLY. The snare around its foot was sturdy, and though the crow had struggled and lamented, it was now resigned to die. Not high above the earth—not even at the place of its own choosing, where it might recite the names of its ancestors. *AllTheJewels, LastToFlee, BornTooSoon, EatsAlone.* No, it would die here, tethered to this crude nest. Proud crow, who'd once known the wend of the horizon and dome of the sky, was now an amusement for any passing creature.

It had discovered the eggs at sunset, pristine and seemingly abandoned. When the snare had tightened, the clever crow had known at once. It had flapped its wings as hard as it could, had hoped to tear the rope from the tree or, if not that, tear its own leg from its body. Maim itself. Leave its gnarled limb behind while it ascended.

The moon was high in the sky. Sooner or later, a predator would come along. Something with hindquarters powerful enough to climb a tree. The crow would've welcomed that fight, but, instead, a pika came to visit. It perched at the base of the date palm and chewed on a lavender sprig. At first, the crow pretended not to notice it. Then, abandoning this ruse, it gave the pika a menacing glare. The pika cleaned its whiskers.

"GO," said the crow.

Yes, it spoke the pika's language. It could only form one syllable at a time, the language of crows being far more ornate, but it was old enough to know all the desert tongues. At the bird's instruction, the pika perked up its ears.

"LEAVE."

In a tiny voice, the pika said, "My brother says he is our mother's favorite, but how can he be when I am last to leave the den? I say this and he bites me on the ear, so we go to her. We say, 'Who is your favorite, mother?' She shows us her teeth and I cower. She says, 'Who? Six leverets in this world, twelve in the netherworld, and you ask me who? I am my favorite—me!' But this makes my brother laugh. He laughs and rolls on his back, so I laugh and roll on my back. 'You,' he says? 'How can you be your favorite? Now tell us who or we will make you bleed.'"

The pika paused to nibble its sprig. The crow had never heard a rodent speak at such length, because it would've been either eaten by now or in hiding. The thought of a meal made the bird's belly rumble. It was rare that the crow, a keen hunter, would deprive itself this satisfaction.

The pika sighed.

"She wouldn't tell us, tree, so he bit her. He bit her on the ear and the tail and also the nose and paws. He made her bleed, but she wouldn't say. I did not bite her. This is my question, tree: because I did not bite her, do you think I might be her favorite now? Or do you think my brother, for being so strong?"

Did the pika not see the crow? Or did it see the crow yet somehow thought it was part of the tree? Before the crow could reprimand it, the pika had flattened itself to the ground and ran in zigzags toward the nearest bush. The crow recognized this behavior as evading capture. Something was approaching.

Even by moonlight, the crow couldn't see very far. Scents and sounds were useless in the air, as they were easily lost on the breeze. The bird moved down the length of its branch, trying to avoid further entanglement. A leopard would be best, it thought, the most efficient killer. Or a pack of jackals. No doubt the crow would be remembered by a different name then—*DiedByManyTeeth* or *TornToPieces*, either of which would confer great honor.

But soon, it recognized its poor luck. Of course, it was the owner of the snare. This person took ginger steps as he walked, as if every shadow were a deep puddle and every stone a slumbering beast. He stopped a short distance away and looked up. Perhaps another bird would've hidden, but the crow had no fear. It opted to intimidate the man instead, spreading its fearsome wings and announcing its presence with authority.

"CAW!"

Much was contained in that one syllable. The crow's name. The name of its father and its father's father. The many animals it had hastened to the netherworld and its own time spent in that place. Of course, the person couldn't understand any of this. In the crow's experience, the human tongue was inefficient, requiring too many syllables to express even the most rudimentary idea.

The man continued to look up. If he hadn't seen the crow at first, he certainly did now. Some time passed, and still, he continued to stare, showing no sign of moving. The crow's wings tired. Eventually it lowered them. It could sense other animals in the vicinity, could feel the warmth of their mammalian hearts and the blood pulsing in their veins. How pathetic they were, to hide. They, too, observed the man from their warrens and dens. But what about this person could the crow sense? Nothing. He stood there like an idol to the gods.

Finally, the man approached the tree. The crow retreated farther down its branch. This time, it *did* get caught in the snare — or doubly caught — and was forced to free its leg with its beak. By the time the task was complete, the man was already halfway up the date palm, shaking the fronds with his effort. Perhaps a leopard would still come along, the crow thought to itself, and catch them both unaware. That idea was satisfying.

When he was close enough to see but not so close that the crow could reach him, the man paused. He supported himself with an arm slung over a branch and his legs hugging the tree. With his free hand, he reached for where the snare had been anchored—again, too low for the crow to reach.

"You're an old one, aren't you?" he said.

The crow didn't respond. There was something unnerving about this person's voice. Perhaps the calmness with which he spoke, or his feigned curiosity. For the first time, the crow experienced a pang of discomfort.

"Old," the man said again. "I can tell from your scars—I can see them better from here. But not so cautious? Those eggs were too good to ignore?"

The crow bristled. It turned to walk away, but the man tugged on the snare, forcing the crow to correct its balance.

"Don't be angry. There's no shame in hunger."

Shame? He would speak to a bird in captivity of shame? The crow opened its mouth to speak, but before it could, the man had started to climb back down the tree. It would have been unremarkable, except he'd untied the anchor and was now pulling the crow through the fronds. The bird could only half-hop, half-fly from one perch to the next as the man made his way, an embarrassment it was forced to endure.

When they'd both arrived on the ground, they stood facing each other. The length of rope was twice as long as the man was tall. The crow didn't know why so much slack was necessary. Perhaps for the illusion of freedom?

The man's skin looked blue in the moonlight. He looped the piece of rope around his hand three times, shortening his leash.

"Come with me," he said. "I want to show you something."

It wasn't a request. Walking more confidently than he had before, he led the crow—again half-hopping and half-flying. The bird knew it was being watched by other animals. It knew it would be taunted for its complicity, but let those who would hide suffer their own indignity. The crow persisted, legs moving, wings flapping. Its body obeyed the man's will even as its spirit resisted.

They were going to the ravine. Man and beast alike had been fascinated by this development in recent days, while birds had scoffed from on high. What was another divot in the landscape? And what about the gods' behavior had been so surprising? They routinely flooded the rivers and directed lightning strikes—how was this any different? In the crow's experience, the gods rarely took accountability for their actions, presuming that their actions *had* any meaning.

When they arrived, the man approached the edge. The crow had hoped he might loosen his grip as he peered over the side, but the human was not so easily distracted.

"You understand me?" he said.

The crow weighed its answer. While doing so, the man yanked its leash again. He pulled so hard that the crow toppled over.

"YES."

"Down there is the netherworld," the man said. "Am I wrong to think so? The gods have created a path for me to follow, and I intend to. You will be my guide."

The crow was shocked, not by the man's assertion, but by his foolishness. Yes, the ravine might represent a path to the netherworld, though whether or not the gods had created it for this purpose was less obvious. Why did the man expect the crow to help? And why travel to the netherworld? Didn't he understand that such a journey would render him dead?

Again, it was impossible to express these thoughts in the human's crude tongue. The crow had to settle for a terser reply.

"NO."

That would be it. Now the man would surely kill the bird. It didn't matter what happened after that. The crow could be plucked and boiled for soup or fed to a dog—neither idea was troubling. It relaxed its wings and waited for the deathblow.

The blow came, but not as expected. The man stared at the bird while he looped the leash around his palm once more. The crow wondered if he'd misunderstood, perhaps substituting KNOW for NO and thus mistaking the reply for an affirmation. Then the man swung the rope. There was no slack. The crow's body was whipped in an arc over the man's shoulder and onto the ground.

The impact was extremely painful. The crow's bones warped and the air left its lungs. Worse yet was the surprise it experienced. Surprise evoked a loss of control, and a loss of control evoked fear, a sensation that was foreign to the bird. While still on the ground, it could feel the man's hands ruffling its feathers in a most vulgar way. Then the crow realized what he was searching for. Before it could struggle, the man had already located its tailfeather.

Having that piece of itself removed was a violation beyond comprehension. The crow wasn't dead, but it should have been. It twisted and flailed. It no longer mattered if its bones ached or its lungs were empty. It made terrible sounds. It told itself this couldn't be happening. In the space of an instant, the crow weighed every decision it had ever made and recognized its arrogance. It felt overwhelmingly sad. If it had been possible to plunge its own beak into its heart again and again, it would've done so—again and again, again and again.

Somehow, the bird's contortions arranged it onto its back, looking up at the man, who was holding its tailfeather. Stiff, stark, and apart."Now," the man said. "You will do as I say."

4

MESHARA

GARASH ARRIVED on the afternoon of the fourth day. Meshara had expected a retinue of slaves and complaints about the long journey—bellyaching to be expected of a man in power. Instead, she was surprised by the modesty of her landlord's donkey. The former soldier remained agile in his middle-age, with only a modest paunch under his full beard. He dismounted in a single, graceful motion and handed the bridle to his attendant.

"You must be Meshara," Garash said, walking toward her. He had the unlucky combination of red hair and green eyes—a warning sign from the goddess Ninhursag, who marked ill-tempered babies at birth.

"And you must be Garash," she replied. For the occasion, Meshara had chosen her finest dress—

linen dyed the color of mint. Though she hadn't had time to bathe, she'd anointed herself with oils and had arranged her hair in an elaborate braid. This ceremony had made her feel like a stranger in her own body, as if she were one of Ziz's ragged dolls. It was both necessary and unpleasant.

Garash embraced her. He said, "You honor me with your hospitality. May An favor you."

"And you," she spoke into his shoulder.

Would her landlord be so affectionate if her husband were present? Meshara suspected not, but the question was moot. She'd spent the past day looking for Temen, but he was nowhere to be found, nor had he left any clue to his whereabouts. Had he intended to meet Garash on the thoroughfare? Was he farther down the ravine? Meshara had questioned Ziz, but her daughter had seemed even more distraught than she.

No husband. No explanation. A farm in ruins and an unknown landlord. If she couldn't honor the debt they owed Garash, he might demand their servitude in return, a common legal remedy. Never before had Meshara feared being a slave, but now the threat loomed. She knew that if she fully embraced the concern, she might cease to function, so she forced it from her brain, like ignoring a dark cloud that hung on the horizon.

"Temen boasts about you," Garash said. "And

you," he added, releasing Meshara and turning to Ziz. "You must be his daughter. I hear only good things."

Ziz blanched at the attention. She had been carefully groomed as well, heeding Meshara's instructions to wear a clean dress. Now she flirted with rudeness, nodding and averting her eyes.

Garash laughed, to Meshara's chagrin. "Mimma— I don't like grown-ups, either."

"You must be tired," Meshara suggested. She forced a smile, trying and failing to catch Ziz's eye. "Can I offer you ale? Will you sit?"

"No. Show me the ravine."

Garash looked at her expectantly. This request was unexpected. It immediately made Meshara feel nervous. No good would come from the ravine.

Meanwhile, Ziz darted away, promptly returning with a goat. Meshara had given her specific instructions, which, in her distressed state, she must've repeated six times. She'd also sharpened the ceremonial blade to a dangerously fine edge. The four of them stood in a bunch—the attendant, too—as their shadows grew long and the goat bleated. Ziz held the animal by the scruff of the neck as Meshara's mouth went dry.

"Garash," she began to say. "There's something you must know—"

"All the way from Nippur, the farmers spoke of it.

They say it opened without warning and goes on forever in either direction. Is that true?"

"Temen is missing." The words dropping from her mouth sank like stones in water.

Garash frowned at her. "Since when?"

"Nearly two days."

"Did he fall?"

"I don't know. Not when it happened, if that's what you mean. But…I can't say for sure."

She watched his face for a response. If only Temen had told her more about their landlord—what sort of man he was and what motivated him—but Temen had never observed others in that way. He had no need.

Ziz struggled with the goat. If she and Meshara were reduced to slavery, their sentence could extend for three years. That was the law as it applied to creditors. Ziz was now ten. The duration of their punishment would see her achieve womanhood, Meshara thought to herself, wasting her best opportunity to find a husband.

Garash stared at his feet. Then he looked up at Meshara, as if seeing her for the first time. "You're scared," he observed. "Don't be. Don't be afraid. Come to me, Meshara. And Ziz. Come—"

Garash opened his arms wide and drew them both in for a suffocating embrace. Up close, he smelled like sweat. Meshara didn't know what to think of his affection. She wanted to allow herself a measure of hope, but she was wary of the man, of his wants and needs and her consequent obligations. Despite his heady embrace, she withdrew into herself.

"There's no reason to be scared," he implored them both. "All is well. You!" he said, ostensibly shouting at the attendant. "What're you doing there? What's the meaning of that goat?"

"For slaughter," Meshara murmured into Garash's armpit. "To celebrate your arrival."

"You honor me again." Kissing them both on the tops of their heads, Garash released them. "Come—let's kill this thing and put your minds at ease."

It would take more than a dead goat to comfort Meshara. She allowed herself only a measure of hope. Was it possible he'd made this journey simply to see the ravine? She couldn't arrange the sequence of events in her head, whether he would've left Nippur before or after the rift had occurred, nor could she ask without seeming impudent. Temen had conceived of the rift as a divine gesture.

Perhaps, if Garash was similarly inclined, he'd forgive any damages to the farm? Whatever his reason for being here, it was his land. He could visit for any reason he liked, at any time.

Unsurprisingly, the former soldier was adept with a knife. As Ziz and the attendant held down the goat and Meshara murmured words of thanks, her landlord severed the arteries in its neck. The animal briefly struggled in Meshara's arms, for it was she who took hold and spoke in a soothing voice, a voice that belied her true feelings. Why did the animal refuse to die? Why could no one do the simple things she required of them?

Only when the goat had been subdued did Ziz impress upon Garash the beer that Meshara had offered him. The attendant took one, too. Meshara encouraged everyone to sit, holding the goat's head over the ceremonial bowl and feeling no more relaxed for the completion of the ceremony, though she was grateful to Ziz for her help.

"You would like my wife," Garash said, making a common assumption among men. Not all women were sisters, just as all men were not brothers. "You two would get along. You're very similar."

"Oh, yes?" Meshara demurred.

"She's independent. Strong. I tell anyone who listens that she runs the household—I'm not embarrassed to admit it."

Meshara smiled. While she very much doubted his wife would appreciate being compared to a farmer, especially one holding a bowl of blood, she knew better than to contradict him. Like all men, he was fragile and would perceive it as a slight, even if Meshara had meant to convey the opposite.

"I'm sure she's impressive."

"You know the law still applies to you?" Garash gestured with the blade, continuing to hold the knife. "Even without a husband. You can still own property, even if Temen did throw himself into the ravine. Is that what happened, do you think?"

Meshara kept her eyes on the bowl. She momentarily felt queasy. The dark cloud on the horizon sounded with thunder.

"I don't know," she replied. "I can't imagine."

"I wouldn't be surprised about Temen going down to the netherworld. His father died last year, didn't he? Fathers and sons have a special bond. Take me and mine. My eldest son is a soldier, like me in my youth. He's in Uruk now, getting his first taste of combat. Before he left, he asked to use my copper helmet for when he sacked the city. 'You mean this old piss pot,' I asked. 'This old, banged-up thing?' I could see how badly he wanted it. It made me proud."

Garash's green eyes were swimming after only one beer. When he laughed, his attendant laughed with him. Meshara wondered if the boy was a nephew, perhaps, or a third or fourth cousin. Garash continued to ignore him, pouring a second ale for himself. Meshara watched the attendant drain his own cup and refill it, trying to keep up.

"Were Temen and Abum like that?" her landlord asked.

"Temen honored his father," Meshara said.

"Yes, but did he want to *be* him? It's not always that way. I hated my father—I can say that now that he's dead."

The goat had been drained of blood. Meshara would have to butcher it immediately, a time-consuming task. She'd planned to show Garash the damage to his property and discuss the farm's future, but he seemed most content in conversation. This, then, would be their new approach; she and Ziz would appease him. Even if Meshara mistrusted Garash, which she surely did, she had to believe that any goodwill generated tonight would be of use tomorrow, when a survey of the farm would be unavoidable. At least they had beer. Temen had left her with that much.

"Take this," Meshara said to Ziz, adjusting the goat in her lap to pass her the bowl. Her daughter lingered at a respectful distance. What at first had appeared to be reticence now seemed deferential. Meshara felt a surge of gratitude. Perhaps she wouldn't have to depend solely on herself? Together, she thought, she and Ziz could charm this man to their favor. This tentative alliance with her child strengthened her.

"Here—see here."

Garash dropped the knife he was holding and removed something from the folds of his dress. Meshara sighed, noting how dirt now clung to the blade. She'd have to clean it again before she butchered the meat.

"Have you seen one of these before?" Garash asked Ziz. In his hand was a stone cylinder, the kind that scribes used to press a seal onto clay. "I think maybe you have," he added.

"It makes a design," Meshara explained, not wanting her daughter to appear foolish.

"Would you like to see it?"

Before Ziz could answer, Garash tipped the ceremonial bowl she held, spilling a small amount of blood onto the ground. Meshara watched as he rolled the cylinder in the puddle and then used the attendant as an easel, roughly spinning the boy to face the other way.

"I can't see," the attendant complained. "What is it?"

"It's a wedding scene," Meshara informed him. Meanwhile, her landlord studied Ziz, who was staring, aghast, at the bloody tableau. Family members gathered around a bride and groom, who were seated at a banquet table. Even from a distance, Meshara could make out their facial expressions—vapid smiles, nothing like real life.

"Have you ever seen anything like it?"

Though the question was intended for Ziz, it reminded Meshara of her own wedding, so long ago. She and Temen had conducted their ceremony at her childhood home. It had been uncommon for the bride's family to host the banquet, but her mother had insisted. Her father had even erected a shrine to the god An, which he'd woven from prairie grass. Temen, who never made a habit of inebriation, had drunk himself ill.

As she gazed upon the illustrated couple, she could still remember the sound of him retching. What did she feel for him now, in this instant? Was it possible to miss him?

"I want to see," the attendant whined, twisting and tugging at the fabric of his dress.

Garash grunted, reaching for his drink. "I'd worry less about pretty pictures and more about changing your clothes. Smell like a goat's blood and you'll attract an Asag."

"What's an Asag?"

Garash grinned at Meshara, who mirrored his smile without thinking. "What's an Asag?" he teased. "What do they teach you in school, besides reading and writing? An Asag is a witch with scales like a snake and claws like a bird of prey. She lays eggs in her victim's stomach. When you hear something on the roof at night, that's probably an Asag, guarding her nest."

"You mean—"

"Yes, halfwit, I mean you."

The attendant clutched his stomach. Meshara felt little sympathy for the boy, who was clearly drunk. He was likely to urinate in his sleep—another mess for her to clean. Still, she retained the awkward smile on her face, even as Garash cuffed him on the ear.

"Maybe we'll find one in the ravine," he chortled. "Maybe it got Temen. What do you say? Shall we go and see?"

"No," Meshara answered him, feeling less rebellious than tired. She'd tried to be as polite as possible, but the weight of the goat was becoming increasingly uncomfortable, and she was further burdened by the tasks that lay ahead of her. The thought of eating made her feel sick, but she knew that she must, whether or not she possessed an appetite.

"First we have to butcher the meat. Then—"

"Hamta!"

Garash lumbered to his feet. Seeming uncertain what to do with his cylinder, he pointed it at her.

"You, butcher the meat," he said. "I'm going to see this ravine I've heard so much about. And she," he said, pointing at Ziz, "is going to take me."

5

ZIZ

THEY LEFT the dwelling shortly thereafter. At her mother's request, Ziz first steered the attendant toward his sleeping mat, the boy being too drunk to find his own way. She then joined Garash to show him the ravine. Meshara had seemed uncomfortable with this arrangement. Ziz's mother had encouraged her to be polite, but not to dawdle.

The sun wouldn't set until later, but long shadows had already been cast upon the ground. As they walked, Ziz pointed out desert animals, but Garash hardly seemed to care. He marched with an apparent disregard for anything underfoot.

"Your mother doesn't know," he said once they'd traveled a short distance. "About the marriage."

These were the first words Garash had spoken to Ziz and they chilled her to the bone. It was true—

she hadn't told her mother, thinking that Temen's disappearance had made it unnecessary. No one else had known about the arrangement but Ziz and her father. Why involve a third person?

Now, Ziz had returned, reluctantly, to where she'd started. Furthermore, she could be accused of lying for having withheld the information. As she walked along the path, her extremities tingled, like her hands and feet had been plunged into cold water.

Ziz looked behind them to see if Meshara was still close enough to hear. Garash hadn't phrased his observation as a question, nor could she think of any advantage to denying it. "No."

"But Temen talked to you?"

"Yes."

"Surely the gods have something planned for you, girl," her landlord said, avoiding a steaming pile of dung as large as an anthill. "To arrange a marriage right before your father dies? Consider yourself lucky —your mother, too."

"You don't know he's dead," Ziz protested, causing Garash to snort. She found it odd to experience anger when, of course, she'd also entertained this notion.

Why deceive Meshara if there wasn't the possibility that Temen was dead? If he were dead, was that a good thing? Did it mean Ziz still had to get married? Perhaps it would be better for her to marry if Temen was gone. Without her father, everything had become unclear.

Ziz glared at Garash. She resented how easily he dismissed Temen, as if her father's life and death had amounted to nothing, yet she didn't belabor the point. "Why didn't you say something?"

"To your mother? I wanted to understand the situation before I did. I still don't know if I do."

They both grew silent as they approached the ravine. Ziz stopped walking before she reached the edge, allowing Garash to continue on without her.

Not since Temen had announced her engagement had she felt so anxious. What would happen now? she wondered. She felt like a trapped animal—thoughts obscured by panic, wanting only to flee.

"Amazing," Garash said. He leaned forward to peer into the darkness. "And it happened without warning?"

"Temen and I were standing there," she replied.

Garash turned with a grin. "No wonder he jumped," he said. "Can't you feel the allure?"

"Don't say that," Ziz protested again, louder than before. Now she felt foolish for having wished her father dead. Here was another man come to take his place, as if she'd traded one undesirable outcome for another. The son, she thought, was likely to be worse.

Suddenly, she imagined pushing Garash.

The idea was seductive. If the ravine had claimed Temen, surely it could accommodate one more person? Who, then, would know of the arranged marriage? Ziz would be free of her obligation, once and for all, and the world would be free of Garash.

"My own sons wouldn't follow me to the netherworld," he continued to say, as if she'd remained silent. "Or maybe my oldest would. But no, I don't think so—they know their worth. They'll mourn for me and honor me, but they wouldn't be so rash. How about you, daughter? How will you honor your father-in-law?"

Ziz was still entranced by the thought of pushing him. She wondered if she was strong enough to do so. There could be no hesitation. She'd have to shove as hard as she could, and only when he was standing right at the edge. What if Garash divined her intent? What was to prevent *him* from throwing *her*? It wouldn't be hard to arrange another marriage for his son.

"You have something of mine," he said, holding out his hand. "The other cylinder. Don't lie—I sent it back with Temen. You've seen it—I can tell." Narrowing his eyes at her, he said, "Give it."

"I don't have it," Ziz confessed. "I threw it away —in there."

She pointed at the ravine, causing Garash to look over his shoulder.

"In there?" he repeated. "Why would you do such a thing?"

The wind came over the chasm and made a growling noise. Sneering at Ziz, Garash turned on his heel and stalked to the edge. This was her opportunity. His back was as wide as a wall.

Ziz had correctly anticipated the end of Garash's life. What she hadn't anticipated was the leopard that sprang out of the ravine and closed its jaws around his neck.

Rearing on its hind legs, the cat was taller than the man, with irregular black spots on her honey-colored fur. It was as if, together, the wind and shadows had achieved mass, brought to life by murderous intent. Garash didn't make a sound—he didn't even register surprise. Rather, he collapsed under the animal's weight, his body jerking as she sank her teeth into his spine.

Ziz dared not to breathe. She dared not to think. She was possessed by a fear more ancient than all her years—a fear that knew the predator from watering holes and open plains, from tall grasses that swayed in a breeze.

Ziz's joints locked in protest. Her shoulders attempted to meet where the ridges of her spine protruded, thrusting her chest forward like a supplicant. The muscles in her neck went taut from adrenaline.

The leopard stared at Ziz with sanguine eyes. She draped a paw across Garash's body in proprietary fashion while grooming her bloody whiskers with the other.

For a time, it seemed as if Ziz's heart had stopped beating. It then revived itself with a newfound urgency, pounding so hard in her chest that she experienced a shortness of breath. More time passed. The leopard stood.

The muscles in Ziz's body remained frozen. From her previous experience with big cats, she knew they would only kill to eat or to protect something, either territory or their young. The leopard hadn't taken a bite of Garash other than her death blow, nor did she seem interested in his corpse, so it wasn't hunger that had inspired her. Sure enough, a cub soon emerged from the ravine. It yowled at Ziz before its mother urged it along.

The leopards stalked past Ziz in the twilight, passing close enough that the ripples were visible across their flanks. The mother's feet padded gently on the ground until they could be heard no more.

Ziz looked to where Garash—or, rather, the body of Garash—lay. It occurred to her that, despite the appearance of the leopard and her cub, nothing had changed. Willing her legs to move, she took one step and then another. The smell of blood was overwhelming—she could taste it in her mouth.

Commanding herself not to gag, she squatted beside Garash and reached for his shoulder.

Despite what she'd thought about pushing him into the ravine, his body proved difficult to move. Nothing seemed to be connected to anything else. His shoulder shifted free of his torso, and he was heavy, heavier than in life.

Ziz struggled to roll him onto his back, after which she was forced to confront his expression—all the horror, unvocalized, now represented on his frozen face. She felt a pang of sympathy for the man, but then she imagined the face of her would-be husband and recalled the stone cylinder. Her sympathy dissipated.

She pushed. Rolling the body, Ziz found it easier to move as she gained momentum until finally gravity took over, claiming first an arm, then a leg, and then everything at once, so quickly that she had to steady herself, lest she follow her father-in-law down to the netherworld.

Ziz rose to her feet. The wind blew across the ravine. She listened for instructions from the gods, as Temen would've done, but there was nothing to hear. So, she ran.

Ziz sprinted for the dwelling. Ahead of her, the sky had turned a deeper shade of blue, nearly cobalt, with the first stars visible on the periphery. She ran as fast as she could, her feet barely touching the ground. Even from a distance, she could smell the roasting goat flesh. The memory of Garash holding the ceremonial blade, the slaughter, and the still-present threat of the leopard all conspired against her balance.

She tripped over a rock and went sprawling.

"Mother!"

Ziz had difficulty getting her legs underneath her. Her vision was filled with prairie grass and red clay until Meshara's hands were lifting her up and she could distinguish her features.

"What's the matter? Where's Garash?"

"Dead," Ziz gasped.

Meshara held her daughter at arm's length. Her face was impossible to read, her eyes flitting from Ziz's face to her now-bloody hands. Ziz pressed forward, wanting only the shelter of her mother's arms, but Meshara kept her at bay.

"Was it you?" she said.

"No! There was a leopard. It—"

"Hamta!" Meshara snapped, giving Ziz a shake hard enough to rattle her teeth. "Don't lie to me. Speak the truth."

"Dead," Ziz said again. But this was the answer to a different question, the question she'd expected to hear from her mother. Meshara seemed capable of accepting Garash's death. It was Ziz's innocence that inspired doubt.

Behind them, fat from the goat's corpse caused the cookfire to pulse. Her mother had chosen to prepare dinner outside rather than squeeze their guests into their modest home. Meshara looked up at the night sky and then back at Ziz.

"We'll be slaves," she said. "He has a wife, children—they'll claim you killed him."

"I didn't!" Ziz protested.

For the first time, she almost told Meshara about the arranged marriage. Perhaps Garash had shared the news with his son or wife? If Ziz and Meshara went to Nippur and presented themselves as the future daughter- and mother-in-law, perhaps they'd be spared?

But still, if Meshara had to be convinced of Ziz's innocence, what sort of ally would she make? Ziz recalled her mother's assurance that she wouldn't have to wed before becoming a woman and felt the sting of that betrayal anew.

"The goddess," Meshara murmured. She was still staring at Ziz, but her mind seemed to be elsewhere.

"What?"

"Ninhursag. Here—you wait."

Her mother slipped inside the dwelling, where presumably the attendant remained asleep. The cookfire sizzled louder than before. The goat was being overcooked on one side.

After a moment, Meshara emerged with a pile of

clothes "Bundle these," she instructed Ziz, tossing the garments at her. She then picked up the bowl of goat's blood. Showing little care, Meshara emptied its contents before the dwelling, all of it. Ziz could hear the earth guzzling the liquid.

"What're you doing?" she asked.

Meshara didn't answer her. Instead, she gathered a handful of barley grain from their evening meal and tossed it onto the roof of the dwelling, handful after handful, making a sound like falling rain.

"Mother?"

"Bundle those clothes."

But Ziz could only stare, so Meshara did the task for her, stretching one dress to encompass the others and tying the arms in a bow.

"We will go to Nippur," she said, speaking evenly. "We will go to the temple and explain your father is missing. We will offer to serve the goddess Ninhursag. And Ziz?"

Ziz was still staring at the roof of the dwelling. Above and beyond, a full complement of stars had established themselves in the night sky.

"Ziz," Meshara said, taking her face by the chin. "We will not speak of Garash ever again."

6

CROW

A BIRD without a tailfeather couldn't fly.

It could remain aloft for a while, but this was similar to a person jumping up and down. A bird that couldn't fly lost touch with its birdness. Such a bird would eventually go insane. It would fail to recognize its own kind and begin to eat stones. This would be the crow's fate if it didn't reclaim its tailfeather.

The man was clinging to a rock face. The crow was clinging to the man. Neither of them spoke. The crow was silent out of spite, and the man was overwhelmed. Terrified, even.

This was to be expected. They were in the netherworld. The cliff from which the man hung was sheer. There were no available handholds, and even if there had been, it would've been unclear which direction would provide safety. In the crow's experience, people always climbed up, even while everything conspired to bring them down.

Perhaps the crow could glide without a tail-feather? There was nowhere to come to rest, however—no solid earth below. Only the clouds and more of the anonymous cliff face, which wasn't really a cliff.

The bird had been to the netherworld twice before, both times with the intent of seeing the gods, if only for its own satisfaction, though on neither journey had it been successful. Only a crow could pass between the two realms without forfeiting its life in the process. The reason for this was known only to the gods themselves. Or perhaps there was no reason, and the gods had made an oversight.

"What is this place?" the man said. "Where am I?"

"HERE," the crow said.

"This isn't what I wanted. Where are all the people?"

"HERE," the crow croaked again.

Indeed, they were surrounded by mitu—above them, below them, on either side. The face of the cliff was covered with people. Every mitu had been afforded a grip and no good way to proceed, though not every mitu had been provided a crow to speak in his ear. Only this mitu, because only this crow had been foolish and weak.

"How can I find anyone?" the man asked.

Was this what he desired? To find someone? The crow didn't properly understand the man's motivation. Though he'd brought them here, the man hadn't stated *why* he wanted to visit the netherworld. Was it to locate an ancestor? The crow's own ancestors were nowhere to be seen, and this, for the time being, was good.

There was a sound from above, which wasn't really above. The crow could guess what it meant—an avalanche of mitu sliding down the mountainside. No, not sliding. Falling. An avalanche of mitu and pieces of mitu—heads, hands, and limbs, still clutching and complaining as they scoured the cliff face, which itself was shaped by a layer of mitu—who either retained their handholds or were carried away. The man tucked his chin into his chest and shut his eyes. The crow took shelter in his armpit, its tailfeather so agonizingly close that it could sense it more than see it.

What effort would be required to reattach a tailfeather? Was it something the crow could do by itself? It had to possess the thing first, that much seemed clear.

The tide of bodies had already diminished, but still the man kept his eyes closed. The crow stretched forward. It extended its body as far as it could reach and then extended its beak, too, straining toward the man's waist, where the tail-feather was tucked, not thinking whether its labors would be observed, not thinking about anything other than a missing part of itself and the necessity of being whole again.

"You!" the man said.

He could only move one hand from the cliff and still maintain his grip. Accordingly, he used his left hand to remove the tailfeather from his waist. The crow would've gasped if its anatomy had allowed it to do so. Instead, it produced a strangled squawk. What if something struck the man's hand? What if he let go?

"NO," the bird protested, the syllable arising from deep within.

"You'd leave me here like this?"

The man seemed offended, as if it had been the crow's idea to visit the netherworld and not his own. The crow spared a glance at the man's face. His skin had acquired a ghostly pallor and his lips were already turning blue. Typical of a mitu; where did he think he belonged, if not here?

Then an idea occurred to the man—the crow could see it in his eyes. With his left hand, he easily folded the feather in two. The quill was pliable—it didn't break, but warped under his pressure. He stuffed the bow-shaped plume in his mouth. Black barbs peeked out between the corners of his lips. It required significant effort for the man to ferry the feather to the base of his throat and swallow it down, an effort reflected in his features as he stared at the crow. The muscles in his neck convulsed. Then the tailfeather was gone.

The crow acted—it didn't think. It pecked at the man's throat. It had no trouble puncturing the skin, but its beak was stymied by a layer of muscle. Already the tailfeather had progressed on its journey downward toward the man's stomach. The crow imagined it. It tried to follow its passage. It pecked at the base of the man's throat and then at his chest, attempting to breach the ribcage. There was no blood to reward the crow's efforts, nor could the man feel any pain. Mitu were denied the grievances of the living; they neither breathed nor ate.

Nevertheless, the man responded poorly. Using the same hand with which he'd mangled the tailfeather, he seized the crow and flung it from his person. The bird fell. It flapped its wings, but they sluiced through the air. It tumbled past clouds that weren't really clouds, through space that wasn't really space, in a direction that was neither up nor down, until it realized all this and felt foolish. It was a new feeling for the crow. Whereas shame had weighed it down, embarrassment was like a bubble in its breast. The crow wasn't falling

—it knew better. Using its beak and feet in combination, it managed to snag upon a mitu. This mitu was in conversation with herself—

"… used one rag for dishes and another to clean the table and floor. I followed her rules—it was her kitchen! I cooked with salt, like my husband preferred. But only she knew the difference between the two rags. They were the same size and color. When I guessed wrong, she called me stupid, and when I guessed right, she scolded me for guessing. I don't understand why there couldn't be one rag for all the things. If everything must be clean, I couldn't understand …"

—but the crow paid her no heed. Because it could sense the distance between its tailfeather and itself, it knew precisely how far it had fallen.

Not 'fallen.' A thing couldn't fall in a place with no orientation.

The prospect of climbing back to where the crow had begun was tiresome, but only if it invoked the specter of gravity. Dismissing all notions of the natural world, it was able to walk over this carpet of mitu, each one engaged in a private torment—

"… even though I fed and bathed it. Perhaps *because* I bathed it—it hated to be bathed. But its fur …"

"… kill you choke you squeeze you 'til your eyes

bulge out your tongue unfurls then rip it from your head ..."

"Third choice is fire. Fourth choice is ..."

"... made the ugliest face while learning to smile. I remember thinking: one must learn to smile? So many things a person must learn, not just walking and talking. Also thinking: you can see the adult face in the face of the babe. But I couldn't see it. Will I? Will she ..."

The crow found the man, still desperately clinging to the wall, now with both hands. The crow was pleased by the damage it had wrought. Blood or no blood, the mitu's wounds were gruesome, providing an interior glimpse of his collarbone and trachea. The crow was determined to do much worse, later. For now, the man possessed a vital piece of itself. No matter the crow's resolve, it was incomplete.

"WHO?" it cawed.

If the man desired to visit the netherworld, he clearly sought an audience with someone. This was what the crow intended to convey. The name of that person should have been on the man's lips, whether it was some distant relative or the recently deceased. What the man didn't know, but the crow did, was that no guide would be required to find this person. Despite its appearance, the netherworld wasn't some vast and vacant place. The man only needed to see beyond his current predicament.

The crow lowered its head so it could peer into the man's eyes. He still looked panicked, probably convinced he'd fall if he let go. Or maybe he was surprised to see the crow again, unable to comprehend how the bird was standing on the cliff face while he, the man, was dangling. Whatever the case, he didn't seem to register the question.

"WHO?" the crow asked a second time. Adding, for context, "HERE."

Now the man understood—the crow could see it in his eyes. It was good they were able to communicate, given the paucity of the crow's human vocabulary. However, this newfound connection didn't foster empathy. If anything, the crow was more determined than ever to pluck out the man's eyes.

"My father," he said. "It is the gods' will that I speak to him."

His father—of course. The man pursued wisdom. How disappointed he'd be.

"DROP."

Here, the crow knew its brevity would be a hindrance. It didn't literally mean *drop,* nor was the man inclined to do so. What it would've said, had it been able, was, release yourself from the idea of up and down—first your mind, then your hands. See this place for what it really is—a cliff that isn't a cliff, clouds that aren't really clouds. Release it all.

It was problematic to fit into one syllable.

"DROP."

There was another sound from above, just as before. A solitary body part rolled past them, like the first pebble in a landslide, except this was the manicured foot of a rich woman. It kicked the man on the crown of his head. The crow understood the result of these avalanches, whether or not it was the gods' intent—they caused the mitu to cling even tighter than before. Rather than questioning where the spills originated from, or what had caused them, they converted all their energy to enduring the onslaught. Indeed, the man had flattened his cheek against the cliff and closed his eyes.

So, the crow attacked. It savaged his hands, taking great pleasure in their leathery resistance. Pain was only an idea, like up and down, an association with a former place. The man's body knew better. The man's body didn't bleed. But as long as he championed these concepts, he would remain bound to them, and thus he attributed pain where he expected to find it.

"Stop!" he shouted. "I'll fall!"

The crow didn't stop. It teased the man's veins like a clew of worms. The man continued to shout, even as the first torsos rolled past him, followed by entire mitu, their voices rising and falling in a litany of complaints. The crow hopped onto the man's shoulder. From there, it was at greater risk of being knocked off, so it aimed its next strike with precision. It pecked at the man's spine, right where the vertebra met the skull.

Involuntarily, the man's hand released.

7

MESHARA

MESHARA WAS VERGING ON PANIC. She had difficulty controlling her voice.

"You must give us something to eat," she insisted for a second time. Beside her, Ziz leaned against her arm. Normally, her daughter would've expressed embarrassment at her mother's outburst, either by rolling her eyes or distancing herself, but now she was too tired to protest. Before them stood a steward of the temple, a young woman who'd chosen to demonstrate her piety by staining her tongue. The effect was disconcerting, like speaking to a serpent with a human face.

"Mimma," the steward said. "I already told you—no food or alms until morning."

"Who's looking for alms?" Meshara snapped.

"We need the goddess's charity. Don't you understand?"

Their words echoed off the high ceiling. The temple of Ninhursag was nearly empty at this hour, with the majority of devotees at home to prepare their families' evening meal. Meshara was confident that, beyond this common prayer area, there must be a kitchen where stewards received their daily rations and a barrack room where they slept. She and Ziz had been denied further entry to the temple. Rather than take advantage of its amenities, all they could do was appreciate the statues of the goddess in repose.

For nearly two days, they'd been in transit. Their only rest had come as passengers, and even then, Meshara had barely slept, neither lulled by the river nor the ruts in the road. She worried Garash's disappearance would be noted, eventually, as would their absence from the farm. What happened next was unknowable. She was tormented by thoughts of punishment, being sold into slavery, or beaten, or sentenced to death.

On that first night, after Meshara had used blood and grain to fake the arrival of an Asag, she and Ziz had left on foot. They hadn't spoken much—they'd been moving too fast to do anything but pant, their breath visible by the light of the moon. This had been the easiest part of their journey. In the past,

Temen had traveled by riverboat to and from Nippur. Knowing this, Meshara had planned to negotiate their passage, but the riverboat captain had been too attentive.

A jovial fellow with a broad chest, he'd observed the family resemblance in Ziz. While Ziz had curled into a ball at the bottom of the boat, Meshara had cursed her luck, and the gods, too, for their apparent sense of humor. What else could explain the man's shrewdness than he'd recognize the similarity between a child's ear and that of a former passenger? In the next bend of the river, Meshara had demanded that they be put ashore, citing the impropriety of two women in a boat with a strange man, as if this arrangement hadn't been clear from the start. She couldn't risk being identified if anyone had spoken to the captain later.

Later the next day, they'd joined a caravan on the thoroughfare to Nippur—an Akkadian merchant and his five brides. Each wife had been assigned a different shade of blue, by which her children, slaves, and possessions could be identified. Meshara and Ziz had been welcomed by the youngest bride, who wore indigo and didn't have children of her own. The other wives had refused to acknowledge her, and even their slaves had been sullen and resentful.

The youngest wife had given them food and new clothes to wear, also indigo. She'd made a bed for Ziz on an ox-drawn cart and had insisted that she rest—Ziz, who quickly surrendered to sleep, though she frequently called out in her dreams, much to Meshara's frustration. The young bride had attempted to befriend Meshara, describing her life in some far-off city-state and disclosing the merchant's sexual proclivities. The man wore yellow, like the sun.

"If only he rose and fell with such regularity," the woman had jested, but Meshara had been reluctant to speak, lest she reveal anything memorable about herself. Conversation had stalled until it ceased altogether. By the time they'd reached Nippur, the caravan undulating like a coral snake, the youngest wife had soured on her, making rude comments to her slaves about the narrowness of Meshara's hips.

The caravan had deposited them at the bazaar. Meshara had been too anxious to ask for directions to the temple, not knowing whom she could trust. She'd also feared losing sight of Ziz in a place so large and hectic. It was frustrating to devote so much of her attention to her daughter. Indeed, she'd clutched Ziz's wrist like a prisoner in shackles.

Eventually, Meshara identified a priest by his red linen robes and had asked for directions. He'd been in the process of haggling over a pestle and seemed vexed by the interruption, but still, he'd set them straight. Ziz had gawked at everything, seemingly overwhelmed by each new sight and sound—exotic fruit, caged birds, and insults passed in a variety of languages.

And now, having arrived at their destination, Meshara could feel the weight of her own exhaustion. She hadn't eaten in two days—her guts were cramped, and she was painfully gassy. If this black-tongued steward didn't acquiesce soon, she was liable to become violent.

"Where do *you* eat?" Meshara asked her. "Where do you sleep?"

"Me?"

"There must be a kitchen inside the temple? Beds?"

The steward stood up to her full height and gave Meshara a haughty smile. "I am a servant of Ninhursag," she said. "The goddess provides for her children."

"Then let us serve her," Meshara practically begged. "Can she not provide for two more? Isn't there enough for everyone? Enough food? Enough space on the floor?"

The steward was about to renew her protest when a third woman joined their conversation. Her garb identified her as a devotee and not another steward—a wealthy devotee, too, judging from her linen. Meshara hadn't noticed her before.

"Hamta!" the woman said to the steward. She

was old enough that her roundness had been replaced by sharp edges. “Don’t be bold.”

“Bold?” the steward retorted. “You have it all wrong, Hazi. I already explained—no food or alms until morning. If she’s too plain to understand—”

This woman, Hazi, surprised Meshara by slapping the steward in the face. It was a significant blow—the impact made a meaty sound. Meshara gasped. Even Ziz was startled from her stupor, staring at this woman who’d suddenly become their matron. The only person who seemed unimpressed was Hazi herself.

To strike a servant of the goddess was to risk Ninhursag’s wrath, though Hazi seemed unconcerned by threat of retribution. Sumerian women were taught from childhood to be demure. Meshara’s own mother had been outspoken in her opinions, though she—like Meshara, who didn’t consider herself meek—had reserved her influence for the family dwelling. Ninhursag herself occupied a private sphere in the heavens rather than competing with the male gods.

Perhaps wealth had made Hazi bold. Meshara wondered what a rich person was doing among devotees, but perhaps she was mistaken—perhaps the older woman spoke to the steward not as a supplicant, but a superior? Whatever the reason for her confidence, Meshara found it alluring—exciting, even. Hadn't she wanted to slap the steward, too? And what had been the goddess's immediate response, if not indifference?

"You hit me," the steward complained. She touched a hand to her face, where her cheek was already turning red.

"I'll hit whoever I want—the High Zagmi can kiss my palm. Can't you see this woman is mourning? Look what color she wears."

Meshara looked down at herself. She was still wearing the clothes given to her by the Akkadian bride, as was Ziz—indigo, to match the youngest wife. Meshara hadn't considered the color's significance when she'd accepted the garb, only that her original dress had been soiled from travel. True, in some remote places, people did wear indigo to connote a mourning period. Alternately, a widow could carry rocks in her pockets, bury a mirror, or fast during the new moon. There was no shortage of ways to signify loss.

Hazi turned to Meshara. "Come with me," she said. "We'll find you a meal."

If Meshara intended to correct Hazi's misunderstanding, now was the time to do it—any longer and an explanation would be required. But why squabble over details, she thought, when Temen was effectively dead? That she hadn't deliberately worn mourning colors didn't alter her situation, and the promise of a good meal was too tempting to refuse.

Together, they crossed the temple floor and walked down a rear staircase. Meshara could hear the steward trudging along behind them. Hazi must've been a person of significance, Meshara thought, if her violence hadn't led to their expulsion. Maybe her husband was an influential man? The steward had called her by name, which suggested familiarity, and Hazi acted as if she knew where she was going, not bothering to see if she was being followed.

Meanwhile, Ziz stumbled to keep up, pressing her cheek against her mother's side. Meshara could smell her daughter's sour-milk breath, like a scent from early childhood—all those hours held captive to a babe's appetite, the chewing and mewling and sweaty closeness. She pushed Ziz away and watched as her eyelids fluttered open, still frustrated by her helplessness.

They arrived at the bottom of the stairs and, soon thereafter, the end of a hallway. There, a door opened onto a dining area populated by stewards. Hazi marched directly to where the meal was being served and inspected the fare.

"Good," she said. "Food." Though the look on her face betrayed distaste for those who would consume such fare, as well as the meal itself.

Meshara went to see for herself after first seating Ziz at a nearby table. The steward in charge of the meal retreated a step. Her tongue was also stained black.

When Meshara peeked inside the pot, she was disappointed by the sight of lentil stew, similar to what she would've served in her own dwelling. Minutes ago, it would've been a welcome development, but now it represented the best the temple had to offer, and a paltry offering at that. Frowning at the grey-brown slop, Meshara imagined the quality of sleeping mat she'd be offered, narrow and unforgiving, in a room occupied by countless other sleepers, muttering and farting the whole night through. No doubt, Hazi slept on straw or feathers. No doubt, her meals were finer.

"Good?" Hazi said again. She looked at the steward holding the ladle, who paused her inspection of her teeth with her tongue.

Meshara made an indifferent sound. "I suppose?"

"Good."

The powerful woman turned to leave. Meshara turned with her. From where she stood, she could see Ziz laying with her head in her arms and the steward from upstairs, her cheek still enflamed where Hazi had struck her. The girl narrowed her eyes at Meshara, as if Ninhursag herself were expressing contempt. Without Hazi's patronage,

Meshara knew they'd be subject to even greater indignities, and Ziz was more of a hindrance than a help.

"Take us with you," Meshara blurted out.

"What?"

"We'll do whatever you want. Please, don't go."

Hazi blinked at her, considering the request. "No," she replied.

When she turned again, Meshara clutched her sleeve, knowing it was inappropriate to do so. "For my daughter," she begged. "Look! How long will they let us stay? A day, maybe, after you leave? Two? Please—are you a mother? Do you have children?"

By now, she had drawn the other stewards' attention. If word of Hazi's intervention hadn't already spread, it would before long. With chilling certainty, Meshara could guess what sort of treatment she and Ziz would receive at their hands. It made the arches of her feet sweat. Hazi had secured their welcome while making them pariahs.

The older woman was appraising the borrowed clothes she wore. Before Meshara could plead again, the matron asked, "Who do you mourn for?"

Meshara considered the question. There was only one answer that approximated the truth, but was it the right one? Or would Hazi prefer another? Temen could be either alive or dead, as the situation warranted. Meshara thought of the path created by a person's lies, so difficult to navigate once embarked upon, and decided to be truthful. Temen was gone. Temen was dead.

"Her father," Meshara said, pointing at Ziz. "My husband."

Hazi's face softened. It was the correct answer. Meshara experienced a wave of relief, but this heady sensation was immediately flattened by the sound Ziz made. Ziz, who moments ago had appeared to be asleep, now raised her head and emitted a wail. Ziz, in whose red-rimmed eyes Meshara could see Temen—not the ears, as the riverboat captain had seen. It should've been a moment of triumph. Instead, Meshara felt only weariness.

8

ZIZ

SHE NEVER STOPPED DREAMING.

Ever since they'd fled the dwelling, Ziz had found it impossible to separate her dreams from reality. During their trip downriver, she'd imagined their boat to be a hollowed-out gourd and the captain to be an enormous spider. In the water, she'd seen faces on the fish, singing songs that couldn't have penetrated the fast-moving surface. And the endless caravan that had spanned from one horizon to another—how could that have been real? In Ziz's mind, the colors had been bold and varied and had provoked familiar associations. Deep blue for the wings of a butterfly, light blue like a barren sky. Yellows like ale, like honey—like the sun.

At other times, Ziz had been visited by horrifying images. The wedding scene from Garash's cylinder—

she imagined the bride and groom with their eyes gouged out. Or visions of Temen falling. Ziz had imagined him clinging to the sides of the ravine, his arms and legs stretched to preposterous lengths.

Worst of all were visions of Garash himself. Ziz could hear the roar of the leopard and the sound of her teeth sinking into his skin, and would know her landlord was close. She'd squeeze her eyes shut, but still he'd come for her, with the same plodding gait and same harsh laugh. Whether awake or asleep, she was unable to hide.

She knew something was wrong with her. It was like being victim to a lingering illness. Had Garash infected her in some way? Or had she left something of herself behind? She couldn't pose these questions to her mother; Meshara had been angry with her ever since the farm, and now she seemed determined to curry Hazi's favor. Ziz herself felt angry, but also scorned. Sometimes the first emotion was louder. Other times, the second, as they competed to be heard.

Hazi's house was large and full of people. Every day, Ziz discovered new rooms, though no matter how far she wandered, another slave would appear to shoo her away.

Hazi was a wealthy woman—Ziz didn't need to be told that. Whereas her home was only one-story tall, she and her husband had expanded outward from their original property, buying the houses to their left and right, as well as the houses to *their* left and right, and had filled their central courtyard with even more rooms, a never-ending series of hallways. Everything was painted white and all the furniture had been made from wood. Every room had at least two exits, sometimes three or four. Occasionally, Ziz would note the absence of a ceiling. She'd be startled to discover a sky full of stars or to feel raindrops on her shoulders.

In all her wanderings, she never once encountered Hazi's husband, nor did she hear his name spoken aloud. The slaves would refer to him as *the master*, gossiping about when he might return or how he liked things to be arranged. Hazi had only intimated his existence. She used the term "we" when speaking of household decisions and never entertained male guests, with the notable exception of the High Zagmi.

Ziz had never met a woman in possession of such power. It made her hopeful and giddy, while, at the same time, inspiring feelings of recrimination for her mother and herself. If it was so easy, what had they done wrong? Meshara was clearly impressed by Hazi, and why wouldn't she be? She followed her around and rarely spoke in her presence, content to listen to the rich woman's musings.

Ziz had also never known her mother to consort

with anyone but Temen. In many respects, Meshara's new relationship had begun to look like a second marriage—partners, but not equals. This made it easier to rationalize Hazi's clout. It also made it easier for Ziz to go unnoticed—not that it was her intention. There was always something to eat when Ziz wanted it. Her clothes were laundered while she slept. If she requested a doll or a distraction, these things could be acquired from the bazaar, though mostly she explored the compound, testing the reality of her situation as best she could.

Her first encounter with Wasu was by accident. Given the breadth of Hazi's domain, it would require three or four visits before Ziz could find her way back with ease. She arrived in a distressed state, convinced she was navigating a maze of the gods' devising.

The first thing Ziz noticed upon entering Wasu's room was the enormous bed. It took up much of the floor and was covered by pillows of various sizes. The next thing she noticed was the boy himself. If the bed owned the majority of the space, then he occupied slightly less.

The fattest person Ziz had ever seen had been at a livestock auction, a woman pregnant with twins, an omen more dire than red hair or green eyes. But Wasu was obese; his flesh seemed to exceed the dimensions of a normal body, like a vessel filled to overflowing. Ziz failed to comprehend how someone could eat so much as to achieve such proportions, or, even if enough food could've been provided, how a person could forgive himself for such greed.

Of course, none of these thoughts occurred to her in coherent fashion. Given her confused state, she was preoccupied by the novelty of the vision. For once, she was almost certain she was dreaming.

Wasu looked at her. He'd been frowning at a beam of light on the floor, but now he smiled.

"What have you brought me?" he asked.

The features of the boy's face were normally proportioned, inasmuch as they were centered amid his gargantuan head. He had wispy hair and pallid skin. Ziz could distinguish beads of sweat on his upper lip.

"What have you brought me?" he asked again.

Just because this was Ziz's vision didn't mean she had agency—the images she conjured did as they pleased, often to terrifying effect. This enormous child was liable to rise up and eat her, which, after all the nightmares she'd suffered, would've come as a relief. Ziz glanced around the room and was surprised to see only one door. Aside from the window, there was no other point of entry. She wondered if they were on the outskirts of the compound, in a room that bordered the street.

"Nothing," she said. "I don't have anything for

you." It felt akin to speaking to herself, but he'd posed the question.

Wasu frowned. "No?" he said. "Why not?"

This question she didn't deign to answer. With one last peek around the room, as if committing the place to memory, Ziz had exited the way she'd come. And that would've been the last time she saw Wasu, had the decision been hers to make. Except, of course, it wasn't.

Henceforth, he began to appear in all her dreams —not only her waking fantasies, when the boundary between reality and fantasy was indistinct, but also those times when she was fully unconscious. Despite his prohibitive girth, Wasu preceded Ziz to the most remote corners of her imagination, from the peaks of Mashu to the muddy banks of the Euphrates River. He always had the same question for her, despite the circumstances, whether she found herself alone or fleeing from danger.

"What have you brought me?"

He was always expectant, never appreciative. The crowded features of Wasu's face could only express a narrow range of emotions, from anticipation to perplexity. Once, Ziz thought he might cry when she refused him, but he only chewed his lip, because she never had anything for Wasu, not even once. Something about his constant request made her angry. It reminded her of Temen, how he would use her to improve his station in life, as if Ziz were just a means to an end. In her anger, she elected to deprive the corpulent boy. But still, he refused to leave her alone.

Even when she was spared his physical presence, he continued to haunt her. In her daily life, Ziz would catch herself asking people, "What have you brought me?" Was this what it felt like to be a man? she wondered.

When the slaves came back from the bazaar, bearing armloads of vegetables and ampules of spices, "What have you brought me?"

Even when a bird or insect visited her room, which she'd learned to identify from the cracks in the ceiling, Ziz would receive her tiny visitor by the window and whisper, "What have you brought me?"

The words, she learned, didn't mean what they professed to mean. It was a recrimination. No one ever brought her anything of value, not when she withheld her gratitude. But the more frequently she asked, the more difficult it was to stop.

The day finally came when Ziz relented. She was in the clutches of a nightmare, trapped inside the dwelling, without Temen or Meshara to protect her.

There was an Asag on the roof. Ziz could hear the sound her talons made as she paced the thatched surface—heavy, like the monster was twice as large as the house. Dust rained down wherever the Asag settled her weight. In the dream, it was unclear if she knew that Ziz was there. Ziz tried to be quiet. She tried to limit her motions, remaining stationary as her heart pounded.

Wasu was also present in the dream; he was sitting on the floor where Temen and Meshara usually slept, wedging pillows from his own bed beneath his knees and thighs. When he saw Ziz looking at him, he stopped what he was doing. He seemed unconcerned by the Asag.

"What did you bring me?" he said.

The Asag paused. The intensity of her listening snuffed the embers of the cookfire. Ziz shook her head. Wasu cocked his head to one side and frowned.

"What did you bring me?" he said again.

The Asag shrieked. She scuttled across the roof, her talons now visible through the weave of mud and prairie grass, spilling sediment onto Wasu's head. He was about to speak again, Ziz could see it in his eyes. With these fateful words, the Asag would come diving through the roof. Ziz had to keep him quiet. She had to give him something.

There was no food; there weren't even raw ingredients to choose from. Ziz looked for an article of Meshara's jewelry, something shiny to catch her eye, but she couldn't spot anything. The Asag shrieked again. The only thing available was the An doll with the missing foot. The figurine was lodged under her sleeping mat. Ziz pulled it out and thrust it in Wasu's face, mouthing the word, *Here*.

The boy looked at the gift. He inspected the god frontwards and backwards, opening and closing his fat fingers around its torso.

"A boy," he said, as boldly as if they were standing two rooms apart. "Like me."

The Asag went berserk.

She started to come through the roof. Ziz fled as far as she could into the shadows, but Wasu seemed unconcerned, still seated in Temen and Meshara's resting place—still clutching the doll. The Asag was nearly upon him. The clamor was so great, it reminded Ziz of the rending of the ravine, a tumult that had seemed to originate from within her.

Then Wasu put the doll in his mouth. First, he attempted to bite off its head, or so it seemed. When that didn't work, he forced his jaw wider and, pressing with the flat of his palm, swallowed it whole. Ziz stared without comprehension. Even as she watched, the Asag stopped screaming. The only sound was Wasu's labors. Once the doll had vanished, he massaged his throat until the passageway was clear. His eyes grew watery, but ultimately, he rubbed his belly and smiled at Ziz.

Then, she awoke.

Immediately, she knew that something had changed. Ziz sat upright, entombed within her blanket, under which she'd rolled off her sleeping mat and across the floor.

From the cracks in her otherwise intact ceiling, she knew that she was back in Hazi's compound, not her parents' dwelling, nor under attack by an Asag. More importantly, she knew she was awake, not dreaming. For the first time in days, possibly a week, Ziz felt herself to be clear-headed.

She burst out of her room and went running through the house. She hadn't been back to Wasu's room since their first encounter and didn't know where to look. Navigating the network of hallways was made even more difficult by her newfound clarity. Every person, color, and sound were rendered in stark relief, demanding that she pay close attention.

Finally, the recipient of good luck, she found her way—the bright room with only one exit. There he was, sitting among his pillows, this immense, doughy boy. He'd been dozing, drooling with his eyes closed, but now he roused himself. Wasu blinked his eyes and gave the same smile as before.

"How did you do it?" Ziz demanded of him, finding it difficult to believe her good fortune. "How did you make my dreams go away?"

The smile left his face. She watched as he licked his lips, wondering if the An doll was still lodged in his gut.

In reply, he asked her, "What did you bring me?"

9

CROW

THE CROW HELD onto the man so they wouldn't be separated. The void they were passing through was impermanent. Once they'd quit the cliff, a new tableau had become necessary. They could've landed anywhere—on hot desert sands or an identical rock face. Instead, they splashed down in the middle of the ocean.

The crow assumed it was an ocean because it couldn't see land. This was after it had resurfaced, its initial fall plunging the bird deep into water that wasn't really water, demanding that it rise like a piece of cork. Even without its tailfeather, the crow was comfortable floating on the waves.

Was the mitu? Apparently so. He floundered a little, but still managed to keep his head aloft. Perhaps he'd learned to swim on the Euphrates River as a child. The surface of the water was placid, the sky above them also serene. Instinctively, the crow spread its wings and fanned the air, but arose no higher for its effort.

"Where are we?" the man sputtered. "What did you do?"

"HERE," the crow said, because they hadn't traveled anywhere.

"There's nothing to hold onto."

"LOOK."

All around them the water was rife with mitu. Some maintained their equilibrium, like the man, but most only allowed their backs and shoulders to crest the surface, while their limbs dangled below. The crow could tell which had been there longest from how bloated they'd become. It assumed there was another layer of mitu on the ocean floor, many bodies deep.

The man appeared surprised by what he saw, then determined. The falling body parts on the cliff face had robbed him of his innocence. He paddled toward a nearby mitu, a woman with skin the color of milk. Her long hair fanned the waves in a sinister corona.

"*You* did this," the man accused the crow, once he'd secured the woman as a buoy. "This is your fault."

"FAULT?"

The crow laughed at the suggestion. It was a terrifying sound, harsh and unforgiving. How could any of this be the crow's fault? Then it remembered its tailfeather and its laughter died.

"You're supposed to be my guide," the mitu said. "Where is my father?"

It was evident the man couldn't see things for himself. He required the crow's help to identify his ancestors, which raised the problem of language. How could the crow communicate with the man, one syllable at a time? The answer was *slowly*, but the crow was impatient. The man's ancestors had to be summoned. This wasn't something the crow could do on his behalf. He had to do it himself.

"CALL."

"What do you mean 'call'?"

"CALL," the crow persisted. The living frequently invoked the dead, whether it was their intention or not, either by mentioning them in conversation or by mimicking a sound or expression. The difference was that here, the dead would answer their summons.

The man looked dubious. How he beckoned his father would speak to their relationship, as would his father's response and how quickly it came. In the crow's experience, its ancestors had arrived with terrifying speed both times. The memory made the crow feel cold, despite the warmth of the sun that wasn't really a sun.

"Abum," the man said. He mumbled the name like a bashful child.

"CALL," the crow berated him.

"Abum!"

The mitu under the man rolled over, revealing itself to be not a woman, but a man. Similar to his son, Abum was skinny and bald, with stern features and a protruding ribcage.

Seawater drained from his mouth. "Who calls?"

The son was horrified, or maybe it was his way of registering surprise. Releasing the body of his father, which he'd so cavalierly made use of, he briefly sank below the surface, only to reemerge a moment later in a panicked fit of splashing. Abum continued to float on his back. To the crow, his penis looked like an enlarged leech—an opportune meal, under the right circumstances.

"Father," the man sputtered. "It's me, Temen."

"I have a son named Temen," Abum said.

"It's me. I came to find you."

The elder mitu performed a sort of roll, submerging his lower half in the water and raising his torso. "A poor excuse for a farmer," he said. "My son, Temen."

Finally, the crow had a name, though one he couldn't pronounce in a single syllable.

Understandably, Temen seemed discouraged by his father's revelation. For its part, the crow wasn't surprised. Conversations with one's ancestors never went as planned; the dead felt no compunction to be polite. Wisdom, when it arrived, was rarely what was sought.

Temen appeared to gird himself.

"Father," he said. "I've traveled to the netherworld to find you. I've used this crow—"

Here, he gestured at the bird, as if an introduction were necessary.

"—to be my guide. I've come to ask you: am I right to marry Ziz to Garash's son? Should I wait for another offer? It seems the gods are trying to tell me something—why else cause the rift at that moment? Tell me what to do."

Another misconception was that the dead followed the affairs of the living. Even now, as Temen floated on the waves, could he see the date palm they'd left behind? Or the ravine, or his farm? How was his father meant to understand this question, unless the events he described had predated Abum's death?

"Temen?" Abum said.

"Yes, it's me."

"How is the farm?"

Temen looked askance at the crow. "The farm?"

"I tried to teach you—I did my best. It was never clear if you didn't want to learn or were incapable. I always suspected the latter. You seemed to resent the land—the land that gave you food and purpose. But your wife—she understood. The daughter of a basket weaver. If I only had one child, why did it have to be you? Why couldn't she have carried my name, or—"

Temen silenced his father by dousing him in the water. He pressed down on the mitu's shoulders, momentarily elevating himself while Abum slipped below the waves. There was no struggle from the old man, nor would any harm come to him—he was already dead. The look on Temen's face failed to connote rage so much as frustration, a crease between his brows and a pinching of the mouth. The crow expected he'd release Abum as soon as his irritation had passed.

During its own lifetime, the crow's father hadn't offered similar criticism, but neither had it offered praise. In fact, the crow had never heard its father speak. It had gone without a voice for so long that it was known by a second name, *SaysNoMore*. Some had claimed it lost its voice in battle with a hawk, while others said the gods had stolen it as a form of punishment. However it had become afflicted, the crow had always assumed there was wisdom in its father's silence. Perhaps, like Temen, it would've been unsettled to learn the truth.

Temen's ire was quick to fade. He released Abum with one final shove, sending the other mitu deeper below, before he fitfully resurfaced, gasping for air he didn't need. Air that wasn't really air. He emerged as a different mitu from before.

An entirely different mitu—the crow was certain at once. This other man was larger than Abum, stockier, and had a wound that spanned from his neck to his shoulder, as if something had taken a bite. Of course, that presumed he'd suffered the injury in the natural world. The crow considered the deeper waters below and suddenly felt wary.

"Garash?" Temen exclaimed, flailing a little himself. "What're you doing here? Where's my father?"

"She fooled me!" the other mitu said. "She knew it was there! She led me to it on purpose."

"Abum?" Temen called out. It had been easier to see when he'd supported himself on the back of another. Now, he tried to peer across the water, which seemed to be getting choppier, scanning the other mitu for signs of familiarity.

Garash continued to seethe. He appeared to be holding an object in one hand, a stone cylinder, which made it hard to swim. "When I get back," he said, his head lolling to one side, "I'll teach her! I'll hang her by her ankles. I'll beat her until my arms tire, and when I do—"

"What do you mean 'get back'?" Temen snapped at him. "Where do you think you are? Teach who?"

"My daughter-in-law."

Suddenly, this new mitu had Temen's attention. "Ziz? Is she here?"

For the first time, Temen seemed to genuinely appraise Garash. It was difficult to do so, with the three of them being pitched more urgently on the waves, the crow included. The bird couldn't guess if this change in the weather reflected a shift in Temen's disposition, or Garash's, or something else altogether. Nowhere were the rules of the netherworld compiled for man or fowl to read. The crow had an ominous feeling.

"What happened?" Temen said.

"I asked to see the ravine. She showed me. She must've known the cat was there—it pounced the moment I leaned over. And, meanwhile, your daughter—"

Garash frowned. With his free hand, he explored the torn skin around his neck and felt the mantle of his clavicle.

"It pounced the moment I leaned over," he said again, more thoughtfully than before. "Where am I?"

Temen turned to the crow. "We have to go," he declared. "Now—we have to leave. If Garash is here—"

"What is this place?" Garash insisted. "What happened to your face?"

Not only had the ocean become choppier, clouds had gathered overhead. Something was happening.

All around them, other mitu were lifting their heads clear of the water and raising their eyes to the storm above. Corpses littered the ocean in various states of decay, all of them silent for the first time in the crow's memory.

This was its opportunity to bargain. Temen wanted something only the crow could provide, and whereas he'd been determined to find his father before, this need was more immediate.

"MINE," the crow said.

It took a moment for Temen to understand. "Your tailfeather," he said.

"MINE."

"Once I'm safe. After you bring us back."

Garash regarded them both. "Where are you going? Back from here?"

That was when the crow saw them, or perhaps it heard them first. Together, they arose from some distant shore that wasn't really a shore, a seething mass of feathers, rotten and decrepit. Some were whole, others were not. They spoke in a tongue the crow was startled not to recognize. Their caws were an assault on its ears. The crow's ancestors had arrived.

10

MESHARA

MESHARA HAD NEVER KNOWN a woman like Hazi.

When Hazi's desires ran contrary to the perceived order of things, she carried on as if the world were at fault and not she. She offered no apologies. She paid what she wanted at the bazaar. She welcomed into her home only those guests who had interested her and turned away the rest. When it came to household decisions, like how to punish a thieving slave or how to raise her odious son, she made her own decisions without seeking outside counsel.

Even in the absence of a husband, Hazi betrayed no weakness, nor did she seem to miss him. She conducted herself as a wholly independent woman and the world accepted her as such.

Meshara admired her freedom; she found it alluring and, at the same time, frightening. What guarantee did Hazi have of her privilege? If someone challenged her, what then? Meshara could only observe and fret. Meanwhile, she continued to wear indigo, promoting the idea that she was mourning for Temen, but otherwise felt herself to be invisible or of little consequence. She had no job, no responsibilities.

Ziz spent her days within Hazi's compound, though Meshara didn't know what she did, nor did it concern her, so long as her daughter remained out of trouble. Her whole life, Ziz had been underfoot—their only child, though Meshara had wanted more. Temen had claimed it was a blessing, that the gods must've reserved a special purpose for Ziz. Meanwhile, Meshara had anticipated the arrival of brothers and sisters, until one day she'd accepted it was the three of them, with nothing and no one to improve her situation.

Spared the burden of parenting, Meshara's days often bled into each other, though it didn't trouble her. She listened to Hazi pontificate as though she, Meshara, were a novice. The older woman addressed her as one would a confidante—or a confidante lacking in common sense, perhaps. Occasionally, Meshara would spare a thought for the farm, their livestock, and their crops. But mostly, she tried to find peace in this new life of hers.

She felt most comfortable, most like her natural self, when she was engaged in physical tasks. There were slaves to cook and clean, but other times, like on this trip to the bazaar, Meshara was able to carry things. Hazi didn't mind—she seemed to expect it. She was hosting the High Zagmi later that evening and her attention was devoted to food and drink.

"Dates, sweet cakes, pickled vegetables—we need a mixture of flavors," Hazi said. "He never admits to being hungry, but he always eats what I give him. Such a pain in the side. He requires a finger bowl at all times to keep his hands clean. Yet you see the slaves he takes to bed—not so worried about cleanliness, there."

Twice, Hazi had made a lewd comment in Meshara's presence—both times, she assumed, to evoke surprise or disgust. To make Meshara feel powerless. Now, as before, Meshara kept her face neutral, unwilling to satisfy her matron's efforts.

Hazi walked briskly between the stalls, her eyes scanning the vendors' wares. She was unreserved in her commentary. Anyone could've been listening as she continued to describe the High Zagmi's flaws.

Meshara, her arms laden with items they'd already purchased, looked at the faces of the people around them, trying to see if they registered surprise, but no one was willing to acknowledge what they no doubt heard. Everyone knew Hazi; no one risked addressing her without being spoken to first.

"Is he allowed to do that?" Meshara asked—meaning the slaves, reluctant to repeat the accusation.

"What a foolish question. Who's going to stop him—those girls, do you think? Chattel, everyone. They probably think it means An favors them. The High Zagmi has as much power as people give him—which is why, I expect, he appreciates me. I treat him as an equal. Also, I remember him as an annoying, little boy."

Hazi stopped in mid-stride. Meshara also stopped, causing the other pedestrians to flow around them.

"We should make him end your mourning period!" exclaimed Hazi.

"What?"

"We should tell him it's been long enough, and you require an exception. How long has your husband been dead?"

Meshara adjusted her grip on the items she was carrying, the rudiments of a meal. How long had it been since she'd last seen Temen? Weeks, perhaps? Normally, a widow would be expected to mourn for a year and a day. Conversely, a man wasn't expected to mourn—or, if he did, only until he found a new wife, however best to mitigate his grief. Meshara imagined Temen mourning for her. The man couldn't cook—he'd be famished by the time he found a new wife. The idea inspired a smirk.

"Not very long," she answered honestly. "Ten days? Eleven?"

"Days?" Hazi echoed. "Not months? Well…it doesn't matter. You can say he was ill for a long time—close to death. Or that you'd grown apart. You were already in mourning."

Satisfied with this resolution, she turned to the nearest stall to inspect the goods on sale. An assortment of burnished copper pots reflected the light of the afternoon sun.

"But why?" Meshara asked.

The older woman looked at her and chuckled. When Meshara failed to register any humor, patiently awaiting an explanation, Hazi picked up a rolling pin and tested its weight.

"Wouldn't you like to wear another color—pink, maybe? Don't you desire your freedom? As long as you mourn, you can't own your own land. You can't spend your own money—you can't even meet in private with another man. Do you really need to earn these things, do you think?"

Returning the rolling pin to where she found it,

Hazi muttered, "Don't think *I'd* mourn for very long. More than once, when Garash has gone off to war, I've told him, stay away for too long and I'll find someone else to raise your sons."

Meshara felt her lungs heave, like when the air went thick before a storm.

"What name did you say?"

But she needn't have asked—Garash's name rang in her ears. Either way, the vendor in charge of the stall spoke louder than she, asking Hazi, "You want to buy that?"

Hazi snapped at him. "Do I look like someone who needs a rolling pin?"

Their conversation progressed no further. Hazi had said all she intended to say and Meshara's attention was now divided. She labored to breathe for the remainder of their trip.

Her matron was married to Garash—Garash was master of the household. Indeed, there could've been more than one Garash in the city of Nippur, but such a coincidence seemed unlikely. Meshara had traveled to the temple of Ninhursag, and there, she'd met the wife of her recently deceased landlord. Surely, the gods had been responsible for that introduction and were now enjoying a hearty laugh.

But what did it mean for Meshara and Ziz? Garash's absence hadn't raised an alarm. According to Hazi, he often traveled for months at a time, and it wasn't unusual to receive no word from him. Only his attendant could provide the details of his trip, and even he didn't know of Garash's death, should he unexpectedly arrive at Hazi's door.

Meshara's secret was safe but precarious. How could she feel secure in her position knowing she was only a puppet for the gods' amusement?

She and Ziz would have to leave. The longer they stayed, the greater the risk of their exposure. But Meshara had to end her mourning period first, as Hazi had suggested. Garbed in indigo, she had no agency. Whatever choices she made for herself and her daughter, wherever she decided to go, she was subject to the whims of men and their interpretation of the law.

In this way, even in his death, Temen had failed her. She resented him anew—even more so for thinking courteously of his mourning period.

When the High Zagmi arrived at Hazi's compound later that evening, Meshara made sure her grieving was visible. She and the High Zagmi had never met before, though she'd been present for a previous visit. On that occasion, Meshara had remained in her room, thinking herself unworthy of such distinguished company, nor had Hazi done or said anything to imply otherwise.

Now she wore all the indigo she could get her hands on. The clothes that Hazi had provided were too elegant for pockets, so, instead of carrying rocks, Meshara found a pebble, one roughly the size of a cherry stone, brushed it clean of dirt, and placed it under her tongue. Her own grandmother had mourned her grandfather in this fashion. The pebble made it difficult to swallow and introduced a foreign flavor to her mouth.

"Please eat," Hazi encouraged the High Zagmi once she'd seated him on a mound of cushions. "I can't remember what you like—I told the slaves to bring some of everything. Can I offer you a finger bowl?"

"A finger bowl would be most civilized," the High Zagmi agreed.

A fleshy man, he had difficulty sitting upright on the plush surface. Meshara could easily envision the annoying, little boy that Hazi had alluded to from childhood.

So far, they hadn't been introduced, nor had the High Zagmi acknowledged Meshara's presence in any way—a sign of deference, possibly, given her attire, but more likely an effect of his station. The pebble in her mouth currently occupied her cheek.

Hazi signaled to a slave, who approached with a bowl of water. Meshara was aware that only the more buxom girls had been tasked with serving food this evening and that their clothes were especially revealing. The High Zagmi seemed to have noticed, too, his eyes lingering where the flesh was most prevalent.

"Tell us the latest news," Hazi said. Her use of "us" caught Meshara off guard. It was the closest she'd come to joining the conversation.

"News of what?" the High Zagmi said through a mouthful of prunes. "I know you don't care about temple politics."

"What about Uruk? Were our soldiers successful?"

"Yes—a painless victory, or so I'm told. Painless for us. I imagine some pains were inflicted on the other side before the day was done."

The High Zagmi guffawed at his own joke. Meshara risked a laugh as well—not easy to do without swallowing her stone. Their eyes briefly met, as the High Zagmi reached for his next morsel.

"Hazi's son is one of the soldiers," Meshara volunteered.

"Yes, of course," the High Zagmi said. "He brings honor to his family and to the city of Nippur. I'm sure you look forward to having him home again, Hazi—and Garash, when he returns from his travels. The house must be quiet without your men."

The way he'd said Garash's name caused Meshara to think there was no fondness between the two men

—or perhaps powerful people were always uncharitable to one another. Hazi made no comment, though she gave a polite smile. Meshara wondered how frequently she entertained the High Zagmi while Garash was at home. The priest considered the foodstuffs before him, a frown on his face, before finally selecting a sweet cake, which he delicately lifted between two fingers.

"Two of my men," Hazi corrected his statement, after a silence had passed. "Speaking of which—Meshara's husband is also missing, though I fear she won't see him again in this lifetime."

The High Zagmi chewed and swallowed. "My condolences," he muttered as soon as his mouth was free of pastry. "I'm sure he's with An now."

Meshara nodded and lowered her eyes. She could feel Hazi staring at her, but lacked confidence in what to say next. She was only a farmer, the daughter of a basket weaver. She was ashamed of her station.

"As you can see," the older woman continued, "she's following custom. I've never seen a more devout widow. Perhaps you can tell her what an appropriate mourning period would be?"

"A year and a day," the High Zagmi promptly replied.

His comment was met with silence. Hazi stared

at the priest, hissing at a slave who chose this moment to approach with ale.

The High Zagmi cleared his throat. “Of course,” he amended his statement, looking at the remainder of his sweet cake, “that’s only a prescription. The mourning period can be longer or shorter, depending on the will of the gods. When did your husband die?”

“I’m not sure,” Meshara replied, the answer Hazi had previously coached her to say.

The High Zagmi sighed. “No? How did he die, then?”

This answer, too, she’d prepared in advance. “He fell into a ravine.”

“The ravine,” High Zagmi said, perking up. “I’ve heard of this. They say the gods split the earth in two like a loaf of bread. And your husband fell in? Clearly it was An’s will that they be together in the netherworld—a great honor for you and your family.”

Taking another bite of his sweet cake, he didn’t wait this time to finish chewing. “Your mourning period is over,” he declared. “Your life may resume.”

Shocked, Meshara looked at Hazi, then back at the priest, who moved closer to the food. The older woman grunted her ascent, signaling for the slave to return with the ale.

Meshara didn't know whether she should smile or genuflect. She knew she should feel grateful, but still, who was thc High Zagmi to award her freedom? That prize wasn't his to bestow. Instead of gratitude, she experienced a wave of resentment, both for this man and others like him. She spat out the pebble from under her tongue and caught it in the palm of her hand.

11

ZIZ

ZIZ'S favorite place was the bazaar.

She loved the swell of bodies, how it moved like a tributary, with whorls and vortices where people stopped to haggle. No matter the weather, vendors arrived early to arrange their wares, rarely assigned to the same booth twice and thus constantly being shuffled.

On every surface was a scale. Spices were sold beside bird cages. Loose fruits rolled free and were stepped on, or picked up and brushed off to be eaten. Slaves mingled with their matrons, who mingled with the zagmi, who mingled with a surprising number of children, who themselves were wide-eyed and opportunistic.

Ziz had first come to the bazaar in search of gifts for Wasu. Already, she'd exhausted the possibilities of Hazi's compound, which were treats from the kitchen or baubles from Hazi's jewelry collection. These things were familiar to Wasu. Ziz wanted to surprise him by offering him something new, something that would make his mouth form a perfect 'O.'

Just as in her dream, he ingested everything she brought him, no matter its shape or size. Ziz didn't understand how he remained in good health, or whether that was her ultimate goal—to render him ill. Until he ate something that disagreed with his stomach, it was a question she didn't have to answer.

From the bazaar, she had already stolen a mouse skull, the dried skin of a rattlesnake, a roll of parchment paper, two foreign coins, a carved box, a comb made from tortoise-shell, weights of all different shapes and sizes, a toy soldier, a plum, a pomegranate, a kiwi, and various other items she could fit in the palm of her hand. Size was crucial, not only because of Wasu's determination to swallow everything, but because she never paid.

She didn't have to steal—Hazi's credit extended to most vendors, and those who lacked her business would've been happy for the opportunity, but Ziz didn't want to owe the rich woman anything.

Unlike Meshara, she wasn't enamored by their matron, nor did she feel any gratitude toward her. It was clear to Ziz that Hazi wanted something, some combination of attention and fealty, as if her household slaves weren't enough. Hazi didn't provide anything without exacting a price, whether Meshara's labor or her pride. It made Ziz mad. If Hazi could be greedy, so could she.

Nonetheless, Ziz enjoyed the thrill of stealing and, more often than not, the subsequent chase. On her first trip to the bazaar, she'd witnessed other children's attempts at larceny. Most were clumsy. They paid little heed to the vendor and other adults, so of course they were caught.

Even before she'd pilfered her first gift, an amulet on a chain, she'd resolved to be more cautious. She would allow circumstance to dictate which item she took, rather than be tempted by the item itself. Despite her judiciousness, the vendor would often spot her. It was only by running between the legs of passing adults that she was able to escape on that occasion and thereafter.

On this day, Ziz was looking for something specific, which made her task slightly more difficult. There was a particular type of berry the temple stewards used to stain their tongues. She didn't know its name, only that it was small and purple. Of course, she could've asked, but ever since Meshara's debasement upon their arrival she'd felt nothing but animosity toward the goddess and her servants. Not that Ninhursag seemed to care. What did it matter if

Ziz knew the berry's name, if she was going to steal it anyway?

The food stalls were located at the southern end of the bazaar where they could remain in the shade. It had been three days since Ziz had stolen anything. Still, as she approached the vendors she eyed them to see if any recognized her.

As a rule, she always stood by an adult. The vendors were less suspicious of a child who appeared to have an escort. Most people failed to notice her or didn't care. The adult that Ziz had chosen for her purposes, an older man who walked with a cane, only glanced at the display and moved on.

"Grain, fruit, tubers!"

Ziz checked to see if the vendor's call had appealed to anyone. A slave stepped free of traffic. Ziz tried to match her step, walking behind her and slightly to the left.

"Grain, fruit, tubers!"

"Those plums you sold me were too ripe," the slave complained to the vendor, picking up a melon and assessing its weight.

"When was this?"

"Two days ago."

"You have to eat them right away," the vendor said. His eyes shifted from the slave to Ziz, then back to the slave. He also picked up a melon.

"Mimma," the slave scoffed. "You think I tell my

master what to eat and when? How about these—are they too ripe, too?"

"My fruit is fine. My melons are fine."

Ziz edged around the slave to stand on her right. The coveted berries were in plain sight—the vendor had piled a few bunches beside his scale. They remained attached at the stem.

"Ask about the weights," Ziz suggested.

"What about the weights?" the slave said. Turning to the vendor with some urgency, she asked, "What about your weights?"

Before the vendor could protest, Ziz knifed out a hand. She grabbed the closest bunch of berries and made a sticky fist at the heart of the cluster. Though the vendor was only momentarily distracted, it was enough time for Ziz to retract her wrist before he could reach her. Pivoting, she dashed away, past the slave—who grunted with surprise—and into the oncoming flow of bodies.

"You!" the vendor shouted. "Thief!"

She didn't stop running until she'd reached Hazi's compound. Entering through the kitchen, she ignored the confused or annoyed looks of the slaves who were busy preparing the midday meal and still didn't know what role she, or her mother, played in the household. Berry juice was running down her wrist. Ziz licked a drop as she skipped down the hall, her tongue going numb from its tartness.

When she reached the door to Wasu's room, she allowed herself a small grin. Predictably, the boy was sleeping. He didn't awaken until she was seated at the foot of his bed. She held the berries now in both hands, a grin spanning her entire face.

Wasu opened his eyes and yawned. A thread of saliva bound the roof of his mouth to his jaw. Ziz had learned that he slept sitting up to prevent bed sores, which were a concern for someone as large as he. She didn't know if Wasu was afflicted by some malady—if that would explain his obesity or why he never left this room. He seemed like a happy child, albeit a simple one.

"What did you bring me?" he asked, rubbing his eyes with his palms.

"Remember I told you about the temple?" Ziz said.

"They turned you out. My mother gave you a place to stay."

"Yes, but do you remember what else? About the stewards?"

By now, Wasu had noticed the berries she was holding. Ziz began to pluck them from the stem they shared, one by one, while a low rumble emerged from Wasu's belly.

"Can I have one?"

"They're not to eat."

"Just one?"

Ziz sighed. "Don't swallow it," she said. "It'll make you sick."

But already he'd snatched a berry from the floor. Immediately upon tasting it, Wasu's eyes grew wide and his lips pinched together. Ziz giggled at his expression. When she'd pulled the last berry from the stem, she separated the bounty into two piles.

"Didn't I tell you?" she said.

"Maybe with some honey," he muttered, spitting out the offending wad. "Or a bowl of cream."

Ziz switched to a kneeling position, bending over the fruit and bringing her face closer to his. "They're not for eating," she said. "Listen—we're going to stain our tongues, like the stewards in the temple. Here's how: you take the berries on this side, and I'll take the other. We put them in our mouths and chew them, but *don't swallow*, okay? Just hold them there, as long as you can."

Wasu didn't seem to be fully recovered. Running his tongue over his teeth, he asked, "Why?"

"That's how it works—the juice stains our tongues. If you swallow, it can be dangerous. Poison."

"But why stain our tongues?"

Ziz frowned at him, frustrated by his obtuseness. "So people know we're friends. So, when they look at us, they wonder what we're doing—like a secret. Don't you want to confuse them?"

Wasu considered her question. "You always say no one knows what you're doing here. Not even yourself."

"Yes, but—"

"I know the slaves ask questions about me—like why I stay inside. Why I'm not a soldier, like my brother."

"Wasu," Ziz said in a less patient tone, lowering her chin. "This is different."

"How?"

"It's supposed to be fun."

The rotund boy considered her words. As she sat back, her knees aching from the hard floor, it occurred to Ziz that this was her opportunity to ask about his condition and why he never left this room. Wasu had raised the subject himself, which meant he was less likely to take offense. Ziz had carried the question with her for some time, but, still, she didn't want to damage their friendship. Before she could think of how to phrase it, he nodded in consent.

"All right," he said. "For fun."

Together, they grabbed a handful of berries from their respective piles. They crammed everything in their mouths, reaching for more berries while trying to prevent the previous handful from escaping.

Ziz's tongue burned. She willed herself not to swallow the juice, which was already tickling her esophagus. Peeking at Wasu, she was delighted by the size of his cheeks. Like a greedy pika, his lips already a deep shade of purple.

Finally, when all their berries had been spent, they sat opposite each other. Ziz couldn't risk looking at him again—she was afraid she'd laugh. Just imagining Wasu as a giant rodent made her titter. And what must she look like? The inside of her mouth felt like a viper's den. Her cheeks hurt and her teeth trilled, and still the juice threatened to leak down her throat.

Sneaking a glance at Wasu, she couldn't help herself—she coughed. There was nowhere for her breath to escape, not out her mouth or through her nose. She gagged once, before spewing the half-masticated berries onto the floor. Wasu helpfully thumped her on the back as she cleared her lungs, snorting and laughing. When she was able to breathe again, she allowed herself another peek at Wasu and erupted in laughter, so ridiculous was the look on his face.

"Don't you need air?" she said. "Spit, Wasu—or chew, or something!"

Predictably, he tried to swallow the contents of his mouth, but his stomach rejected it. So Wasu, too, vomited up the berries. Ziz looked at the mess they'd created on the floor. A slave would have to clean it up. How nice that responsibility wouldn't fall to her.

"Did it work?"

Wasu stuck out his tongue at Ziz. She'd never realized how short it was, barely extending past his lips, but the stub that protruded was, indeed, stained —so dark it could've been mistaken for black.

"Yes!" she exclaimed. "How about mine?"

She stuck out her tongue as far as it would go. She was able to measure her success from the expression on his face, a blend of awe and excitement.

"Black like a leech! Mmllaaaaaah!"

This last utterance was accompanied by his own tongue being thrust out, his mouth wider than before, to expose the appendage to the base of his throat.

"Mmllaaaaaah!" Ziz echoed her friend, opening her own mouth wide.

"Mmllaaaaaah!"

They continued to do this for another minute or so, their eyes shining bright, until a slave entered the room, perhaps alerted to the mess by some preternatural need for cleanliness. When she saw the children's tongues on display, she shrieked, covering her mouth with both hands and running out the door.

Ziz and Wasu, caught by surprise, turned to each other and dissolved in hysterics.

12

CROW

THE CROW'S ancestors were getting closer. The murder, this angry congress of birds, appeared to be growing in size, filling more and more of the sky. The crow could distinguish individual voices and understand some of what they were saying—

"CAW CAW"

"THIS THING FROM MY EGG. IN MY NEST. BIRD BUT NOT CROW. NOT BLACK—WHITE. I PUSH IT FROM MY NEST. ALL THE WAY DOWN IT CRIES. MINE? THIS THING? WHY DO I PUSH? WHY DO I CRY?"

"CAW"

"CAW"

—but these words, it realized, had been spoken in the human tongue. Why couldn't it comprehend its own language? Because it had lost its tailfeather and some portion of its crowness? And why did Temen and Garash seem oblivious to the threat?

"Is it yours?" Garash was saying. "This crow? It can take us both."

Temen wasn't listening. Whatever he'd heard in regard to his daughter had rendered him unsympathetic.

"You want your tailfeather." Temen addressed himself to the crow, bobbing on the waves. Even in the diminished light, his transformation was plain to see, his skin pale and his lips the deepest shade of blue. Temen was no longer a living person.

"MINE," the crow responded, urgently.

"Take me back and you can have it."

The crow didn't trust the man, but what was the alternative? Perhaps he'd be true to his word. There was no way to know until the deed had been done and he'd been safely delivered to the natural world.

But now, the murder had arrived. The force of their wings ruffled the already-turbulent waves. They'd come to punish this transgression, a bird in the human morass of the netherworld. A pet, in essence. The murder plummeted, mocking the crow as they passed, each one singing a syllable in turn—

"SONG"

"BIRD"

"SONG"

"BIRD"

—diving into the water and emerging, diving and emerging, whistling past in a fine spray. Soon, once it had been sufficiently debased, they would attack in earnest, plucking out the crow's feathers and stabbing with their beaks.

For one crow to be brought low threatened the honor of all crows. Such a transgression deserved to be punished. Though the crow's ancestors were mitu in their own right, *it* was still very much alive. Unlike Temen, the bird could experience pain.

Temen and Garash continued not to notice. Because they registered no threat, the murder was invisible to them. The crow paddled closer to Temen. It kicked its legs and used its wings as oars. The attacks were getting closer now. It could sense a decision being made.

"OPEN," the crow said.

Temen frowned.

"YOUR. MOUTH. OPEN."

The command couldn't have been clearer; however, because Temen didn't understand, he hesitated. He may even have clenched his jaw a little tighter.

"OPEN."

"What's happening?" Garash said.

The next bird clipped the crow's wing. It cried out in pain, holding the injured appendage to its body. For the first time, Temen saw the murder above them.

"What—"

The crow took advantage. It flung itself out of the water. It couldn't rise very far, but still it was able to achieve the level of Temen's face, which was barely above the waterline. The crow dove for his mouth.

A hasty intake of breath rushed past as the crow squirmed over his warm, plump tongue. It could sense the man's surprise from the tension in his jaw. Following the current past Temen's tonsils and down his throat, it folded its wings against its sides and squirmed forth. Ahead, daylight peeked through the wounds that the bird had previously inflicted. Soon it would be past the esophagus and into the emptiness beyond.

It wasn't easy. The crow was a substantial bird. But, it thought to itself, at least it was safe here from its ancestors. Suddenly, it felt something clutching its feet. A hand? Was it Temen, trying to remove the bird? No, somehow it knew it was the other man, Garash. He wasn't trying to impede the crow's progress—rather, he was pulling himself along. The crow imagined the stone cylinder passing through the narrow aperture.

The muscles in Temen's throat continued to urge them along. Like the rise and fall of the waves, the undulations surged from top to bottom, ferrying the crow and its passenger—the bird's feathers sleek, its eyes useless in the dark—until they passed the last narrow enclosure.

Into the space between.

The crow could no longer feel the man accosting it. Indeed, it could no longer feel its own leg. In this space between the netherworld and the natural world, there were no bodies to be troubled with. There were no oceans or cliff faces, only the notions of things.

"What is this place?" Garash said, his voice appropriately awed.

"YOU SHOULDN'T HAVE FOLLOWED ME HERE."

Did Garash realize how unusual it was for the crow to speak at length? In this place, the bird was no longer constrained by its anatomy.

"What have you done to me?" Garash protested. "Why can't I see anything?"

The crow's blackness matched the blackness of the realm. The crow was everywhere and nowhere at once. It could cross to the natural world, but first it had to summon the notion of Temen.

"Bird! Speak to me!"

"HOW DO YOU THINK OF YOURSELF?" the crow said. "AS A MAN OR A CHILD? IN ONE PLACE OR MANY DIFFERENT PLACES—DIFFERENT TIMES, DIFFERENT SELVES? WHERE

DO IDEAS GO WHEN YOU AREN'T THINKING THEM? DO YOU CARRY THEM AROUND IN YOUR HEAD OR DO THEY VANISH ON THE BREEZE? ARE THEY YOURS? ARE THEY *YOU*?"

"What does that mean?" Garash sounded scared.

"IN THE NETHERWORLD, YOU ARE RESPONSIBLE FOR YOUR OWN SHAPE. BUT THERE IS NO ONE TO BEHOLD YOU. THINK HARD, GARASH—THINK ABOUT WHO YOU WANT TO BE. SOON I WILL BE GONE."

The crow had never done this for another living creature—only itself. It began with Temen's most striking characteristics: his bald head and long limbs. Also his eyes, which were dark and humorless. Once the crow had identified these features, it focused on the sound of Temen's voice; not as he'd sounded in the netherworld, but as the crow recalled him from the date palm, full of malice. A voice purporting to be the bird's master.

Its concentration was broken by Garash, who sounded less aggrieved than before. "Bird," he said. "Do you see me? I remember myself as a soldier. I had the most glorious helmet; it shone like the sun when I wore it to battle. Can you see me now?"

The crow tried to ignore him. Still cradling its half-formed notion of Temen, it shied away from Garash's voice. What else was there to include? The crow's tailfeather, of course, lodged in Temen's belly.

It imagined it there and then wondered if it could imagine it back on itself. The bird summoned its notion of itself, but found that its tailfeather remained unattached, regardless of thoughts of wholeness and flight. It appeared that this piece of the crow, once removed, wasn't so easily replaced. The crow felt a pinch of disappointment.

Its thoughts returned to Temen. There was now enough substance to this notion to produce a drag when the crow moved toward the natural world. It suddenly occurred to the bird that, just as it was missing a piece of itself, it could deprive Temen of something, too—leave something behind. It gave the crow a thrill, this hint of disobedience.

"Bird!" Garash exclaimed. "I've done it. Do you see me as I once was? There's no one as fierce. This is how I want to be remembered. Bird? Are you there?"

"I AM LEAVING YOU," the crow informed Garash. "YOU WILL BE ALONE. IF ANOTHER CROW PASSES THROUGH THE SPACE BETWEEN, PERHAPS IT WILL BRING YOU BACK. I CAN ONLY CARRY THE NOTION OF ONE PERSON. RETAIN THIS IDEA OF YOURSELF SO THAT YOU MIGHT BE SEEN."

"What?" the man said. "What do you mean? Bird—bring me back! Don't leave me here!"

But the crow had already departed.

First, it imagined its own outline, where it began and ended and what constituted its crowness in between. By doing so, it was able to distinguish the blackness of its feathers from the limitless expanse beyond.

Slowly, the void began to fill with artifacts of the natural world. Stars appeared, one by one, and with them a sense of orientation. The sky was up and the crow was down. Next, a landscape to occupy the foreground—the peaks of a distant mountain range and the rows of a nearby orchard. While this change occurred, the crow retained its notion of Temen. It concentrated on the man's outline. As the sun rose on the natural world and the shadows retreated to reveal rocks, clouds, and the occasional scuttering animal, Temen's form remained stationary on the ground.

The crow was proud of its efforts. It momentarily felt guilty for having left Garash behind, but it had been the mitu's decision to follow them there. Overall, the crow was tired but satisfied. Surely it had earned its tailfeather back from Temen, who, even now, was beginning to stir.

"MINE," the crow said again to remind him of their bargain.

Temen groaned. He coughed, licked his lips, and rolled onto his side. His skin was ashen, a contrast to the rich, dark soil. All around them, insects were absorbing the sun's early rays, while plants sagged under the weight of morning dew. The crow could see the injuries to Temen's neck, having retained these details in its notion.

"Where are we?" Temen asked, straightening his legs. He looked like a person waking from a deep sleep, not a man returned from the dead.

"HOME," the crow replied, though this was only true in a relative sense. They were no longer in the netherworld, but this orchard was far from the place where they'd started. The crow couldn't be certain, as it was more comfortable assessing distances from above, but it believed they were closer to Mashu.

At that moment, it heard something it couldn't possibly have heard—the angry caws of its murder. Immediately, the crow looked upward, fearing an impending strike, but there was nothing to see—only the stately progress of a few swollen clouds. Its ancestors had remained in the netherworld, content to have driven him from that place, though never truly content. Might this be the first sign of madness?

"My penis!" Temen wailed. "Where did it go?"

The mitu was no longer prone. Rather, he stood and stared down the length of his body. Where his sex organ used to be, there was now only a smooth patch of skin from his belly to his anus.

The crow would've smiled, had it been able to do

so. This was the part it had deliberately left out. And why not? Temen had no use for it now, being a mitu. And besides, what could be more ridiculous than a human penis?

"What did you do?" the man accused the crow. He was searching the ground at his feet, as if his sex organ might've fallen off.

The crow couldn't help itself. It knew better than to antagonize him, but the opportunity was too tempting. It hopped a step closer. It made sure it had Temen's full attention.

It said, "OOPS."

13

MESHARA

MESHARA ONLY REQUIRED the High Zagmi's blessing to end her mourning period. She could perform the ceremony without him, though Hazi would play a role. Some women conducted the ceremony in public, but Meshara preferred privacy.

First, she didn't belong to an intimate community. Second, she wasn't entirely sure that Temen was dead. He had to be—it only made sense that he was—but she wasn't inclined to taunt the gods.

Typically, the ceremony would also require Ziz's participation, as she was Temen's progeny and had also mourned his loss, but Meshara didn't ask her. The two rarely saw each other or even spoke anymore.

Meshara suspected she should feel guilty about this, but no guilt was forthcoming. Thanks to Hazi's largesse, Ziz wasn't required to perform any chores. Her comfort was all but assured, so she spent her days doing the gods knew what.

Meshara was mildly resentful of her carefree existence. *She* at least earned her way, in service to Hazi. Ziz had befriended Hazi's son, with whom she shared a common laziness. And apparently they'd stained their tongues. The laundry slaves had gossiped to the kitchen slaves, information being a slave's only currency, which they were all too eager to spend. Weren't those berries supposed to be dangerous? If Meshara was being honest with herself, she didn't care. The question of guilt resurfaced. What she truly felt was apathy.

For the previous three days, the logistics of the ceremony had taken precedence over everything else. Hazi had many ideas—about which rooms should be utilized, about what food should be served, about what time of day it should transpire. She wanted to invite guests, but Meshara held firm on her wishes. Predictably, her matron's role had grown from witness to facilitator, but this was also easier for Meshara. After all, there was only one outcome that was important to her.

"The law says I can own my own land?" she asked Hazi as the two women arranged the table. The older woman was moving items to the floor to make space for the tablecloth. Meshara followed suit.

"Unless it's changed since the last time you asked."

"But is it widely accepted? For instance, if you had a farmer and his wife on your land, and the farmer died, would you let his wife stay?"

As she spoke, Meshara inspected the blade she would use. Traditionally, if the deceased were a male, he would've been buried with his favorite knife; therefore, the one used for the ceremony would be of inferior quality. Since Temen hadn't been buried, and since none of their knives had made the journey to Nippur, Hazi had loaned Meshara one from the kitchen. There was no doubting its sharpness.

"The law is the law," Hazi said. "There's also a law that says you can't murder anyone, but it doesn't stop people."

This was not the answer Meshara had been hoping for. Putting down the knife, she said, "Yes, but if you had a farmer and his wife on your land—"

"I don't know," Hazi interrupted her. "Can the wife turn a crop?"

Meshara answered the question as if it weren't rhetorical. "Yes. She can turn a crop."

"Then, I suppose…yes, I'd let her stay. *We* would let her stay."

The reference to Garash made Meshara lower her eyes, a flutter of anxiety tickling her throat. His name was invoked so infrequently that, on occasion, she managed to deny his death. Of course, that didn't change the reality of the situation—that Hazi's matronage would be forfeit, were she to learn the truth.

"You're thinking I should be in mourning, too," the older woman said, intruding on her thoughts.

"What? No—"

"Every time Garash leaves, the slaves gossip. Or maybe they're smarter than that, but I hear it in the bazaar. That he misses being a soldier. That, one of these days, he's not coming back."

The older woman unfurled a tablecloth, which Meshara caught and smoothed out. Rather than steer the conversation back to her rights as a free woman, she held her tongue, if for no other reason than to appear respectful.

Hazi grunted. "This should make me feel bad? Don't come home, I say. I've got my sons—I can run this household as well as he. Maybe I *should* mourn. If he's not dead, let him prove it."

"Could you?" Meshara asked, thinking this might be another way to test Hazi's sympathies.

The two women inspected the tablecloth. Clearly, they'd spread it out the wrong way—both ends of the table remained exposed, while the fabric hung limp over the sides. Exchanging a frown, they rotated it.

"Why not?" Hazi replied. "What would anyone say? Do you realize, if the whole world thought Garash was dead, I could manage our affairs? Not just the household—I'd be in charge of the land we possess and whom our sons marry. Don't you think I'd do a better job than he? He doesn't give it a minute's thought. Instead, he takes out his old helmet and wears it around the house, talking about the time he killed six Urukians before his midday meal. *I* could kill six Urukians before my midday meal!"

Meshara provided the chuckle that Hazi had solicited, but still, she pressed the issue. "Could you?" she said. "I can't tell if you jest."

A smile played across Hazi's face. On this day, she wore yellow, not blue—a color that made her skin look jaundiced to Meshara's eye. "What is mourning?" the rich woman said. "And for whom do we mourn—the gods? Or so a stranger can know I was a good wife? No, we mourn for ourselves. Going from living to dead is easy—first you're one thing and then you're another.

"For those who stay behind, it's not so simple. We must experience the death and wait for it to sink in. Food doesn't have any flavor for the longest time. Conversations seem pointless. The very fact of life is an insult, like your suffering doesn't matter to anyone at all. So, when does the change finally occur? When are the dead truly dead? Only after we traversed the space between."

The idea of mourning for herself made Meshara feel unsteady, like she might suddenly be overwhelmed by the weight of her grief. The distance between Temen's death and her acceptance seemed very great indeed—if he were, truly, dead.

Again, the two women stared at the tablecloth, which still failed to cover both sides. It was clearly a square, whereas the space they were trying to cover was a rectangle. Hazi dropped her end in frustration.

"Mimma," she sighed. "It's a new table. Do you mind?"

"Not at all."

In silence, they replaced the items from the floor. Meshara arranged the blade on her end, where it loomed in plain sight.

"Forgive me," Hazi said.

It was the first time she'd ever apologized in Meshara's presence—certainly the first time she'd apologized to Meshara.

"Forgive you for what?" Meshara said, perhaps a little more aggressively than she'd intended.

"I shouldn't be so cavalier. Today is the end of your mourning period. What I think about my own husband has nothing to do with yours. Still," Hazi said, "don't be surprised to see me in blue."

"I'll tell the laundry slaves to give you my old clothes when I'm done with them," Meshara teased.

Hazi wrinkled her nose. "Wear your old rags?" She scoffed. "Don't be ridiculous. I said I was in mourning, not a beggar."

The two women grinned at each other and then inspected the table. Everything had been attended to—all that was left was the ceremony itself.

Meshara felt a thrill in the roof of her mouth. Or maybe she was mildly nauseated—she couldn't tell which. As Hazi had said, it was unusual in this life for a transition to be so easily identifiable. Meshara's wedding. The day Ziz had been born. Here was another change, after which nothing would be the same.

Hazi sighed. "I wish you'd let me invite people," she said. "There's still time. We have so much food."

"No," Meshara said, eyeing the knife. "Let's do it now."

"You're sure you don't want your daughter to be here for this? She should see her mother being strong."

Meshara shrugged, rejecting Hazi's overture. "Can you find her? Anyway, she has her freedom—what does she care about mine?"

There were no more words to speak—the ceremony itself was straightforward. Using the knife, Meshara would cut off the tip of her pinkie finger, severing the bone at the smallest knuckle. She would perform this act of self-mutilation on her dominant hand, thus representing the part of herself she'd lose forever. In older, less civilized times, a woman in mourning would've been expected to amputate her whole hand, but such an injury would make her a liability and otherwise reduce her value to a future husband.

"Do you know what you're doing?" Hazi asked.

"Of course. Like bleeding a goat."

"I forget," the older woman said. "You have experience with such things."

She smiled, but her face looked pale. Meshara ignored it. She couldn't focus on the task at hand and also comfort her matron.

Picking up the knife, she tested its blade again—as sharp as its form would allow. The secret, she knew, was to find the gap between the bones and to cut as decisively as possible. Any hesitation would result in additional pain and blood, which could cloud a resolute mind.

"Are you ready?" she said.

She didn't wait for a reply. Notching the blade where the digit hinged, she pressed with all her weight. Immediately, she knew she'd missed the spot—the knife slipped down the slope of her bone before it found an opening. With a force of will that seemed to originate from somewhere else, Meshara pressed even harder, feeling the tension in her shoulder and bicep until the metal had passed through, requiring only a quick sawing motion to severe the skin on the other side.

Quickly, she grabbed a napkin to staunch the blood. The tip of her pinkie lay on the table alongside the knife. Later, she would have to make a decision—she could preserve this symbolic piece of herself, or she could ingest it. The latter practice was more common on a farm, mostly because it was unwise to attract scavengers.

Making a fist around the napkin with her left hand, she picked up the finger and stuck it in her mouth. Meshara didn't mind the taste of blood, but its shape reminded her of the mourning stone under her tongue. After a moment, she spat it out.

"No?" Hazi said, some of the color having returned to her face. "I can't say I blame you. We'll put it in salt. You should make your daughter carry it around for a while."

The older woman seemed to have recovered relatively quickly. Meshara felt queasy. The foreign object in her mouth had upset her stomach, and now she could feel her injured hand throbbing. She looked for a place to sit. Spying no chairs, she settled on the floor.

"How would that work?" Hazi mused, "Make her

wear it around her neck? Ha—think what they'd say in the bazaar."

"You said," Meshara began to say, but she had to pause. Closing her eyes, she took a deep breath.

"Are you all right? Do you need another napkin? Something to eat?"

Meshara focused on the rhythm of her pulse. "You said, if there were a husband and wife—on your land—"

"Yes?"

"—you said you'd let the wife stay."

She had to forcefully expel the words, fighting back a wave of nausea. When she opened her eyes again, Hazi was squatting beside her, another first for the matron. The look on the older woman's face was equal parts confusion and concern.

"Yes," she replied. "I did—I'd let the wife stay. But can I recommend something? Maybe eat a fig?"

14

ZIZ

ZIZ HAD BEEN FEELING FRUSTRATED. Wasu had become less and less enthusiastic about the gifts she'd been giving him—acknowledging them, yes, and even eating them, but doing so obediently, like he was accommodating her.

He no longer asked, "What did you bring me?" Instead, he'd take an item in hand, stare at it for a moment, and then place it in his mouth. Upon doing so, Ziz would catch a glimpse of his stubby tongue—still partially discolored, though more plum now than black.

Even more frustrating was the fact that she cared. Who was Wasu? she often asked herself. Some fat boy in a secluded room. What did it matter if he liked her gifts or not? Why, in fact, did she even bring him gifts? Her debt had been paid, if she'd ever owed him.

Yet, she continued to scour the bazaar for new and exotic diversions or returned with items he'd enjoyed in the past. A ripe quince. A polished amethyst. It didn't matter what she found—the act of handing it over divested the gift of any value.

After her most recent trip to the bazaar, she'd have to look elsewhere for inspiration. Ziz had called attention to herself in a way that wouldn't soon be forgotten.

It had happened when she'd tried to steal a hare. There was a vendor who always boasted two or three. Ziz had overheard him explaining his logic to his stall mates, who—having endured his success and now feeling jealous—had ceased to pay attention, which only made him raise his voice louder.

"I had the idea," he said while picking his nose, "that a live animal would sell better. A dead hare just hangs there. Its muscles look slack, and it makes the customer think of chewy meat. A live hare looks far more delicious."

The vendors on either side of him sold textiles and crockery. As she had many times before, Ziz wondered why *they* didn't also sell hares. The animals in question were contained in a wicker basket, balanced on the countertop. It was the only way to advertise his wares, the vendor's tiresome tale notwithstanding.

Ziz inched closer. By proximity, she associated herself with a man who was inspecting household rugs, counting the knots in each tassel. Anyone who glanced their way would've assumed they were father and daughter and that her eyes, along with her attention, were drifting.

"Imagine my surprise," the vendor said, "when a woman asked about keeping a hare as a pet. 'A pet?' I said. As a child, I never dreamed of keeping a pet. There were animals that worked and animals you ate, often one and the same. But trust rich people to complicate matters, turning food into pets. So, yes, I said, 'I can make it a pet.' And charged her twice as much. And she paid! Rich people, I tell you."

In retrospect, it seemed obvious what would happen next. Ziz hadn't expected to pluck the hare from the basket; sticking her hand into all that fur and finding something to grip had been unappealing. No, it had seemed more prudent to tip the basket, free all the hares, and chase one down in the ensuing madness.

The vendor continued to flatter himself with tales of his success. Ziz held her breath. She took another step toward the booth and reached forward. No one paid her any mind until she upended the basket, at which point people paid more attention to the hares, who were eager to escape. She might've caught one, too, had she not been snagged by the one person she'd thought she could ignore—her faux father, no longer busy counting knots.

"It was her," he announced, seizing Ziz by the wrist and hoisting her arm in the air. His grip was painful. Her heart began to race, as the vendor and his two stallmates, still trying to corral the hares, spared a glance in her direction. She'd never come this close to being caught before.

"This one did it," the man said again. "She knocked it over—I saw for myself."

Ziz turned to look at him. He was ugly, with an unkempt beard and watery eyes. She could feel his fingers pressing into her wrist. The man drew her close and talked down to her, his breath reeking of his midday meal—turmeric and onion.

"Was that your plan, thief?" he accused her. "To steal the basket?"

The idea was so ridiculous that Ziz started to laugh. All this effort for a basket? This one basket, amid the hundreds of others at the bazaar? What would she do with a basket?

She could see her laughter had agitated him. He tightened his grip and brought his face even closer. She squirmed to free herself, to no avail. It frightened Ziz. This emotion was louder than humor, louder than contempt, a warning that hailed from deep within her. No one knew who she was. They wouldn't consider Hazi's reputation until it was too late. Men like this, like Garash or her father, were capable of sudden violence, and Ziz had the misfortune of being a target.

The man's face loomed.

She acted without thinking—she jabbed a thumb in his eye. However, her finger sunk deeper than she'd expected. Ziz could feel the curve of the man's eyeball, this orb set deep inside his skull. Her thumb had entered close to the nose, high in the cavity, and suddenly she realized the power she held.

There was no decision about what to do next. The decision lay in her awareness of her power, as if, like the vendor had said, they were one and the same —animals that worked and the animals one ate.

Pressing deeper, she forced the man's eyeball out of his head.

He'd yet to speak during this part of their exchange—everything had happened too fast, coupled with the chaos around the hares. The man screamed. He released her wrist.

His eyeball, free of its socket, remained attached to his head by a raw-looking tendril, which he seemed reluctant to touch. The man drew another breath and then screamed even louder, not bothering to form words, expressing a horror so deep that it stilled the commotion al around them.

Ziz didn't look at the vendors. She didn't look to see what other people were doing. She took one step backwards and then another, and then she turned and ran.

There were many different routes back to Hazi's compound. Ziz didn't think as she ran—or, rather, she didn't consider the necessity of running. She was haunted by the man's face, now with only one eye. Was there a way to replace a person's eye? If it was still connected by its tendril, did that mean he could see? Ziz imagined the eyeball as a separate entity, as if it were floating above the bazaar, watching her, as she weaved between matrons, slaves, and stalls. She felt ill from what she'd done, the sense of power having dissipated like smoke. There was no hiding from the eyeball's gaze.

She entered the compound through the laundry room, where slaves were hanging sheets to dry. Ziz became entangled in one such sheet. It wrapped around her and drew itself tighter as she struggled against it.

"Hamta!" a female voice yelled. "Look what you've done!"

A patina of gore was smeared across the fabric.

When Ziz was finally able to free herself, her first sight was of the sky above, in a room with no ceiling. A half dozen other sheets walled her off, all of them hanging in mute consternation and smelling faintly of citrus.

Ziz located a door. She tumbled down one hallway and then another. By now, she was able to find Wasu's room without thought. The walls of the compound felt similar to those of the alleyway, like she'd never left the street. There would be no safety, neither here nor anywhere else, a feeling she'd carried with her ever since they'd arrived in Nippur, if not since they'd fled from the farm. The eye would find her. But if anyone could avert their gaze, it was her friend.

Finally, she careened into Wasu's sanctuary. As always, he was seated on the bed, though he appeared more alert than usual, almost like he was expecting her. Despite everything else, Ziz waited for the familiar words. When she didn't hear them, when he regarded her in silence, she launched into an angry tirade.

"What do you want from me? I try to please you —I tried to bring you a hare."

"A hare?"

"A rabbit, you fool! I tried to steal one, and when that didn't work, I had to poke out a man's eye to escape. You don't know how dangerous it is, Wasu. All you know," she said, making a sweeping gesture, "is this."

Staring at her hands, he said, "Did you ..."

Ziz looked where her friend was looking, then sputtered with rage. "No!" she bellowed. "No, I didn't bring you his eyeball, you disgusting creature! Is that what you want? Parts of a person's body? Why not mine? Do you want *my* eyeballs? How about my tongue? Maybe you can swallow the rest of me!"

Exhausted, she slumped against a wall. Ziz leaned back until she had sunk to a seated position.

If Wasu felt chastened, he didn't show it. The air was hot. She could smell the tang of his sweat.

"What did it feel like?" he asked her.

She presumed he meant blinding the man. Ziz sighed, knowing she'd answer him—that this would be her offering, however unsatisfactory.

"Good."

"It felt good?"

"He wanted to hurt me," she clarified, drawing one of her legs beneath her. "I didn't let him. That felt good, defending myself. But scary."

Wasu grunted. He scratched an itch on his knee. "No one could hurt me—no one could find me," he said. "I've never done anything like that."

"I have," Ziz said.

Had she? The words had come so naturally. She'd rolled Garash into the ravine. In a way, that had signaled the end of his life. Perhaps Meshara could've revived him. Perhaps he'd still been alive.

Even if the leopard had pounced on him, it had been Ziz who'd delivered Garash to his fate, so—again—she was responsible.

Wasu was staring at her, so Ziz summoned her courage. "Another time," she said. "A man who visited our family. I sent him to the netherworld."

"Did he do something to you?"

Ziz thought about the cylinder Temen had presented her with—the wedding scene. "He wanted to," she said, folding her other leg and sitting up straighter. "But I didn't let him."

Wasu grunted again. "My father is in the netherworld."

He made this statement with a curious lack of sentiment. Ziz had never heard him talk about his father. Obviously, he had one—Hazi hadn't produced Wasu on her own. But for all the slaves' talk of the master, Wasu was always mute on the subject, making no allusions to his family. No one had ever suggested that the master was dead. Ziz would've recalled.

"Did he die a long time ago?" she asked.

Wasu shrugged. "I don't know. I don't think *he* thinks he's dead. I see him in my dreams, but I don't talk to him. Do you know what it's like, there, in the netherworld?"

Ziz shrugged.

"Not what you'd expect," Wasu said with a

grimace. "Everyone talks too much. Maybe we could get a crow to bring us."

This suggestion came as a surprise. It was the first time he'd proposed an activity that the two of them could share, no matter how far-fetched—the first time he'd intimated leaving his room. Ziz's cheeks grew warm with excitement.

In the hallway, she thought she could hear an argument brewing. Had someone followed her home from the bazaar? If so, Hazi would take care of it. Ziz was in no danger of being punished now that she was here.

Meshara would likely scold her for risking their safety, but perhaps not. Ever since they'd arrived in Hazi's compound, Meshara had abdicated most, if not all, of her parenting responsibilities. It didn't matter—Ziz could speak the words without feeling remorse. She could even apologize to Hazi while affecting the same numbness. Anyway, Wasu's comment had inspired an idea.

"I could tell my father," he was saying. "Wherever he is—I could tell him he's dead. The thing is, I never really liked him much, anyway."

"Wasu?" Ziz said. "Tell me more about the crow."

15

CROW

THE MAN WAS DETERMINED to cover himself. He didn't want anyone to see the place where his penis should be, not even the crow, who, having made its joke, had ceased to care.

The bird watched in confusion as Temen experimented with different-sized leaves. For the longest time, it had assumed that humans' garments were akin to feathers, a layer of insulation that sprouted from their skin. Only when it had seen a woman laundering her clothes by the Euphrates River had the crow appreciated their folly.

"Did I leave it in the netherworld?" Temen said. "Can we get it back?"

The crow snorted, a sound that emerged from its beak. "NO," it replied to both questions.

Temen had located an appropriately sized leaf. In

truth, any leaf would've accomplished the same purpose, since he was attempting to cover a thing that didn't exist. This leaf was oval-shaped and conformed to that particular region of his body. Holding it in place with one hand, he used the other to shield his eyes against the sun.

"Where are we?" he said.

"HERE."

Now it was the mitu's turn to snort. "Where's here?" he demanded. "Where's Mashu?"

Together, they scanned the horizon. The crow spotted the mountain first, its diminished eyesight still superior to Temen's.

"THERE."

It pointed with its beak. Instinctively, it motioned to flap its wings and assume a perch—perhaps the branches of a nearby tree, burdened with over-ripe fruit. Temen had made no mention of the crow's tail-feather, nor had the bird asked for it yet. It wanted to appear gracious.

"West," Temen murmured. "More than a day. I'll need a mule."

"MINE."

Temen frowned. "You want me to give you something? After what you did? It seems I should keep it —it's only fair."

"MINE," the crow repeated.

"This isn't even the right place. You were

supposed to bring me home. And what about my father? You didn't warn me he'd be like that. You've been no help whatsoever. But maybe if you help me now...maybe I'll give your feather back."

The crow was astounded—insulted. It didn't trust the mitu to keep his word, but what other choice did it have?

Temen shifted the concealing leaf to his other hand, sparing a look down at himself. "I need clothes," he muttered. "I look—"

His skin was as pale as cream. His lips were sapphire. There was a ragged hole in his neck from which his voice echoed, like he was in constant dialogue with himself. His chest didn't rise and fall. He didn't blink. His entire demeanor evinced a person who was no longer alive. Any beast could've smelled the process of decay from a mile away.

"I look lost," he said, completing his thought. "Which way to the nearest dwelling?"

The crow was no more familiar with this place than the mitu. Still, it ventured a guess.

"WEST?"

Together, they turned their backs on the rising sun. Even though the crow couldn't keep up, Temen refused to carry it on his shoulder, so the bird hop-flapped at a fitful pace, always keeping the mitu in sight while taking breaks.

The apple orchard had been arranged in rows

with ample space given to each tree. The branches reached for the sky like fingers from an open palm, with fruit the size of a child's fist. The mitu tried one and declared it too mushy, spitting it out, though the crow wondered what had inspired him, since he didn't possess an appetite in the first place. The crow itself was famished, but there was no time for food, lest it fall behind.

Instead, the bird imagined eating parts of Temen —his earlobes, toes, or buttocks. There was a certain satisfaction to fantasizing his consumption, no less so because he'd already consumed a piece of the bird. Would the mitu feel anything? If the crow pierced one of Temen's eyes, would the dead man flinch? Such questions, though amusing to consider, were irrelevant to the crow's hunger, which only knew want. Its stomach voiced an urgent complaint.

Eat grass—do it. Look for bugs. Bugs mistaken for sticks. Eat bugs and *sticks. Eat mushrooms. Spoiled apples, rotten stuff. Frogs—oh, if only there was a frog. A hoarse, slippery frog—choke it down like a greasy bubble. Or a pika, its heart still beating. Whiskers to tickle your throat. Fragile bones. Organs like tiny beans. Eat beans—why not? Beans, seeds, faraway smells. Memories. Eat yourself from a time of plenty. Eat the living and the dead. This mitu, who would set a trap for you. And you, you stupid bird, who never expected it. Eat your shame. Your hate. So much. Can you eat it all, you vile creature? Eat, eat, eat.*

When Temen spoke, the crow didn't hear his words. The man was too far away and facing the wrong direction. But then it realized he was addressing another person.

Farther down the path was a small dwelling, and sitting in front of the dwelling was a farmer.

The crow could identify the man's vocation from his clothing. He was dressed for hours spent in the sun, more of his skin covered than the bird was used to seeing, with a wide, floppy hat to conceal his face. He appeared to be mending a ladder that had been lain across his thighs.

Temen spoke again and the farmer stood. The ladder fell with a clatter.

The farmer turned and ran. Temen took a step or two in pursuit, and then seemed to consider the outcome of such a chase.

Spinning to face the crow, who maintained a considerable distance, he shouted, "Fly after him!"

This was presented as a reasonable idea. The crow spread its wings to stroke the air, to pummel, rise, and wade. But a moment later it remembered. Why should it help, even if it could?

"Fly!" the mitu shouted again.

He came shambling down the path. The crow watched him approach with a stomach not much larger than an acorn. It thought of its tailfeather—whether it provided Temen with any sustenance.

All at once, the mitu had eliminated the distance between them and was reaching down to seize the bird. The crow panicked, flapping its useless wings in alarm. The memory of the man's touch was immediate, like the removal of its tailfeather was still happening. Like it was always happening, *would* always be happening.

The man threw it. Immediately, the crow assumed a shape of least resistance. It raised its neck and angled its beak toward the sky. It tucked in its legs. It was flying, up and away, its wings folded against its sides until their use became necessary, until momentum had stalled and gravity asserted itself. Then, the crow pumped its wings and flew.

The experience didn't last long.

It was falling; it could neither steer nor keep itself aloft. The distance it had traveled was a testament to Temen's strength, but now the bird came crashing down through the branches of a nearby tree. It landed under an avalanche of apples—like the mitu parts tumbling down the mountain, thought the crow—and wished, not for the first time, that it was also dead. Free of pain. Free of shame.

Temen came running over. The crow could hear his approach. He was shouting, upset. But then the crow heard another noise—the sound of feet striking the ground. It was impossible to guess how many, but it was more than one person. The crow considered raising its head to see, but decided not to.

"You there," commanded a voice. Everyone stopped running. The voice came from the bird's right.

"Hello."

This second voice belonged to Temen, to the crow's left. In it, the bird recognized something it hadn't heard since their arrival in the netherworld—alarm.

"What...are you?"

Now the bird was sufficiently curious to raise its head, and, with that, the rest of its body, bruised and aching. No one paid it any heed, as a small mound of apples spilled.

Temen cleared his throat. "My name is Temen," he said. "My father's name was Abum. We come from not far away—south, but still in the shadow of Mashu. I was—"

"You're a mitu," spoke the largest of the three men. The crow identified him as the voice from before. Though the bird wasn't adept at reading human faces, this one wore an expression of considerable scorn.

"I'm not," Temen said.

"You are! Look at you!"

Temen made a show of doing so—taking a step back and angling his chin toward his chest. He spread his arms wide to appraise his body, as if there were nothing to give a person pause, neither his coloration nor his injuries.

"Where's your dangle?"

It was a second farmer who posed this question. He pointed, and the others stared. In making himself available to their inspection, Temen had exposed the seamless patch of skin where his penis used to be. He brought his hands together to form a carapace.

"Where's your dangle?" the first farmer echoed the second.

The crow thought he sounded angry. To the extent that it had difficulty translating faces, it could divine their tones of voice, not only loud versus quiet, but nuance. The second farmer had spoken with a lisp. It made the crow think of a snake, replete with darting tongue. The third farmer, whom Temen had initially stumbled across, had yet to speak. He continued to wear his hat pulled low.

"I come from not far away," Temen tried again. "More than a day's walk from here. But if you could loan me a mule, I'll bring it back as soon as I'm able. Please. It's the right thing to do."

The thought of Temen leaving stirred the crow to action. It hadn't been able to keep up on foot—there was no way it could pace a mule. The bird hopped forward, drawing attention to itself.

"MINE."

The men turned at the sound. The farmer with the hat on reached for the larger man. He spoke in the man's ear, words intended to be private. The ladder that had once laid across his lap remained on the ground.

The first farmed nodded. "Your family," he said to Temen. "Do they miss you?"

"How could they not?"

"But are they *looking* for you? How long have you been gone?"

While the first farmer presented these questions, the one in the hat left the group. The crow watched as he began to untie the leather straps binding the ladder's rungs to its stiles.

Temen frowned. The crow could guess what he was thinking—about the netherworld, trying to gauge how much time had passed in that place. "Hard to say," he replied. "Where I've been—"

"But you say a day's journey?"

"Yes."

The two men advanced on Temen. The crow witnessed this development as ominous. The mitu also seemed wary, though he offered a guarded smile. Perhaps he believed they would assist him? People, like animals, often saw or heard what they wanted, whether it be an offer for help or an unguarded nest.

"It's the right thing to do," Temen said again.

Rather than answer him, the farmers positioned themselves on either side of his person. The second farmer, who'd made the observation about Temen's penis, clutched him by the shoulder and elbow. Still, the mitu continued to smile, looking less confident than before. His hands remained over his groin like a shell guarding a snail.

"You've got a way with birds," the first farmer said, nodding at the crow. "Maybe you can tell them something for me?"

16

MESHARA

When it came time to leave Hazi's compound, Meshara couldn't find Ziz, nor did she know where to look. It had been weeks since she'd last seen her daughter or, indeed, since she'd given any thought to how Ziz spent her days.

When Meshara summoned the image of her daughter, it was lazing in their vegetable garden, ignoring whatever task Meshara had assigned to her. The girl had a talent for disappointing her mother, rivaled only by her powers of procrastination. Meshara halfway expected to find her counting flower petals or discerning shapes in the clouds.

Instead, she caught Ziz stealing food from the pantry. Meshara had been reluctant to ask the slaves for help. On the whole, they still treated her with disdain, a show of disrespect that rankled her. She'd been unable to quiz Hazi, lest she betray her intentions, so she'd opted to wait on the outskirts of the kitchen, the one place that everyone passed through at some time or another.

It was shortly before the midday meal when Ziz had entered from the outside, raising the additional question of what business she had to conduct beyond the compound. It was vexing that a girl so young could operate with such impunity—that she had no higher authority to answer to. The only time Meshara left the compound was to carry Hazi's groceries.

Ziz didn't wait to be acknowledged by the slaves, nor was she. It was obvious they intended to deny her presence, a slight that further provoked Meshara.

There were three of them in the kitchen, all female. The cook was roughly Meshara's age. She wore a constant scowl on her face and had hands strong enough to choke a man. Her assistants couldn't have been much older than Ziz. No conversation was allowed to take place as they brought their tasks to completion, but they revealed their age in different ways, chewing on their hair one moment, admiring their reflections in the cookware the next.

Meshara watched her daughter from across the room. Was it possible she was only ten? Additional years seemed to have accumulated. In her heart,

Meshara felt the distance between them. It inspired a dull sadness, this gulf.

She watched as Ziz leaned against the wall and grinned with satisfaction. She seemed to be playing with something under the folds of her dress, but Meshara couldn't see what. When her daughter felt herself to be sufficiently rested, she pushed off the wall, making no effort to avoid the kitchen slaves, nor did she have to. They parted before her like a foul breeze, keeping their eyes on their vegetables or the flour they sifted. The cook's scowl deepened. Humming a song to herself, Ziz plucked a carrot from a cutting board and took a bite. She disappeared inside the pantry.

Meshara could feel a slow creep of exhaustion rising to her temples. Not only did she have to abandon the safety of Hazi's compound, she had to do so in the company of a stranger. Would there be time to mend her relationship with Ziz? Did she even *want* to? Whether or not they left as intimates, they had no choice but to flee. Hazi would eventually learn of Garash's death. If the gods had conspired to bring them together, sooner or later they would reveal the tragic details—why else go to all the trouble? Meshara flexed the fingers of her right hand, noting the abbreviated digit.

Ziz had done this. And now it fell to Meshara to save them both.

By the time Ziz emerged from the pantry, Meshara had positioned herself in the doorway. Her daughter was carrying a handful of almonds. For the briefest of moments, she appeared surprised to see her mother, her face becoming at once young and vulnerable. This expression promptly faded.

"Mother," she said. With her free hand, she popped an almond in her mouth. The other hand remained in the folds of her dress.

"We need to talk."

"So talk."

Undoubtedly, their confrontation had already been noted by the cook and her assistants—the manner in which Ziz and Meshara addressed each other, their hushed tones of voice. The only thing the slaves wouldn't register was the kitchen as their venue. To those who worked here, their domain exerted the strongest gravity upon the house. It made sense that wayward parties would be drawn to them.

Meshara couldn't risk being overheard. Taking a step forward into the pantry, she forced Ziz backwards. Her daughter required no additional cajoling, perhaps conditioned by her father's temper. The room was easily as large as Meshara's dwelling with Temen. Shelves of dry goods extended from the floor to the ceiling. Shelves, yet another sign of Hazi's wealth.

"We're leaving," Meshara said.

"Take something," Ziz suggested. "They won't stop you."

"Not here. Hazi's compound—Nippur. We're leaving the city."

"*We*? I'm not going anywhere."

"Hazi is Garash's wife."

Meshara watched for a response, wondering how much Ziz had already learned on her own, but her daughter maintained a controlled face. Whatever thoughts occurred to her would transpire in secret.

"Sooner or later, she'll figure it out," Meshara continued, speaking quietly. "Where he went, what happened to him. Even if his attendant is no longer there—which, where else would he be? The blame will fall on us. When that happens, we need to be very far away."

Ziz adjusted her posture. Her scowl had become unconvincing. "Where?" she said.

Meshara had given this question some thought. Caravans were always traveling through Nippur, trading whatever goods they carried, acquiring more supplies and moving on. Perhaps she and Ziz could join one. If necessary, Meshara could offer herself as a bride; the loss of a finger didn't make her less appealing. She'd even given thought to a religious pilgrimage, though their treatment at the temple had made her reluctant.

"It's not important. It only matters that we go."

"So, not home?"

Meshara blinked. Why would Ziz want to go there, after what they'd fled from? Home, as she thought of it, was no longer home. Didn't Ziz realize this?

"No."

Ziz folded her arms across her chest. "Not me, then. You're free do what you want, but I'm not going."

Meshara noted her emphasis on the word 'free'—it sounded like censure. She felt a bloom of indignation. "Of course you are. You have no choice."

This was a bluff. She could no more command her daughter than she could make the three women in the other room abandon their stations. Her words had no clout. But perhaps Ziz was still young enough to believe her mother's authority was absolute. What was power, after all, but misplaced confidence in a parent, or anyone else?

And what about Hazi's compound might appeal to Ziz? Her friendship with the boy, Wasu? The shelves towered over them on all sides, creating a sense of vertigo. Meshara kneaded her toes against the rough-hewn floor. Nothing about this place was inviting.

"You don't have a choice," she said again.

"I've been promised."

"Promised what? Who promised you something? Whatever they said—"

"Temen arranged a marriage for me. With Garash's son. The soldier."

Meshara felt her legs go weak. She had no place to store this new information. If her mind were arranged like the pantry, the fact of her daughter's betrothal didn't fit beside anything else, and neither did the memories of their life before nor her notion of what was yet to come. Temen had made an arrangement without consulting her? He'd chosen a match for their daughter without confiding in his wife? When had he planned on telling her? How long had Ziz known? How was it possible for Ziz to possess this information, but not Meshara?

"What?" she said.

Her daughter was watching. Gone was the adolescent from before. Here was a woman exerting a newfound confidence upon the world. Under that confidence, Meshara knew, abided a helplessness—a suspicion it might be for naught, that intent and righteousness weren't enough. Meshara had experienced this helplessness, too. But rather than be moved toward empathy she allowed her anger to overwhelm her.

"Why did you keep this from me?" she snapped. She didn't care if the slaves heard her. Soon enough, everyone would know. Meshara grasped Ziz by the shoulders. "Why didn't you tell me immediately?"

That was all it took—the woman was gone and the adolescent returned. Ziz shrugged her off. In the confined space, she looked feral, angry enough to bite.

"What does it matter? *You're* free to go."

And with that, she brushed past Meshara. Through the open doorway, the sounds of the kitchen slaves had ceased. There was no noise from the alleyways outside. In fact, it was so quiet that, had she listened carefully, Meshara might've been able to hear imperceptible sounds. Air circulating from high to low. The beating of her own heart. Silt.

There were few options available to her; she could do as Ziz said—she could leave on her own. Was Meshara prepared to abandon her daughter? What sort of man would Ziz marry in her absence? What sort of life would she have?

Perhaps, if they had this conversation again, Meshara could convince her to go, this time choosing her words more carefully. Though the question remained: if Ziz had been promised in marriage, what were the ramifications if they fled? Did Hazi know about the betrothal? She couldn't—she would've said something to Meshara by now.

That was her first order of business, Meshara decided—to tell Hazi. The powerful woman would respond in one way or another and subsequent decisions would be made.

The kitchen slaves had conspicuously resumed their labor by the time Meshara passed through. Even the cook looked more abashed than dour. Meshara considered the time of day and where she was likely to find her matron. It was too late for a trip to the bazaar. She'd probably be in her suite. Only yesterday they'd entertained the High Zagmi there, another costly affair with exotic dishes and comely slaves. Perhaps Hazi would be picking at the remains.

Meshara found her with little trouble. Hazi was standing in front of her mirror. Large and ostentatiously framed, it was the only mirror Meshara had ever seen before. When she'd first encountered her own reflection, she hadn't recognized herself, nor had she warmed to the experience, which felt like a kind of sorcery. She'd learned to avoid the foggy glass, fearing, and even loathing, the image that resided there. Hazi, in contrast, made a regular study of her own features. Even now, she was considering herself in profile.

"I'm thinking of growing it long," Hazi said, presumably speaking of her hair. "Like the women of Kish—have you seen them?"

"I have something to tell you," Meshara said. She was resolved to share the news before she could reconsider. "My daughter has been promised in marriage to your son, by their fathers. This is what she tells me."

Hazi found her eyes in the mirror.

"Garash was involved?"

Meshara nodded. "This is what she tells me," she said.

Hazi turned around. Meshara wondered if Hazi would actually grow her hair longer, and if she would be compelled to do so too.

"Remind me her name again?"

"Ziz."

Hazi nodded. "Ziz. So Ziz is to be married—"

"To a soldier," Meshara completed the thought. "She claims that Temen—that was my husband, Temen—and Garash reached an arrangement. Temen told Ziz, but he didn't tell me. If I'd have known, I would've told you sooner. I would've—" Meshara sighed. "I don't know what I would've done," she confessed.

Hazi smiled, a smirk that affected the corners of her lips. "What's to know? You would've planned a wedding—nothing could be easier. Only, not to a soldier."

Meshara opened her mouth to protest, but Hazi's smile expanded. "Garash is blessed to have two sons," she said.

17

ZIZ

THE CONVERSATION with Meshara had rattled Ziz—there were too many unanswered questions. Would her mother actually leave her here? Would she tell anyone of the arranged marriage? What would happen if she did?

Ziz wanted to trust her, but she still felt the sting of betrayal, first at Temen's appropriation of her future, then at Meshara's lies about womanhood. Ziz wanted to push these thoughts as far away as possible.

Luckily, she had the perfect distraction. She'd acquired her most recent gift for Wasu not at the bazaar, but from a peddler, the former being too dangerous to risk. A crow's tailfeather wasn't the kind of object she could expect to find for sale among the kitchenware and produce. If it were being sold, it would be found among the other novelties.

Thc peddler Ziz had visited had been hawking his wares for three days. He was shorter than Ziz; his yellow teeth were on prominent display and his beard was a mixture of grey and orange hairs. Each day, his sampling had grown smaller. Soon, Ziz suspected, he would sell his last item and move on.

In the doorway of a potter, the vendor had laid out a mat and carefully distributed his goods so that no object competed with its neighbor. Once, Ziz would've happily offered any of these trinkets to Wasu—a copper goblet, carved playing dice. But now, she had a particular gift in mind.

She hadn't seen a tailfeather, so there wasn't one to steal. It also meant she'd have to speak to the man, though she'd scoured his inventory on the second and third days, in case she got lucky. By now he'd come to recognize her, clucking his tongue in exasperation as she perused his goods yet again.

"Is it the mat?" he finally said.

"What?"

"You look so hard—I thought maybe you wanted the mat. It's for sale, too. Would you like me to clear the merchandise so you can take a better look?"

"I don't want the mat." Ziz scoffed. Then she looked to either side of them, before inquiring, "Do you have a tailfeather? From a crow?"

As far as she knew, it wasn't illegal to possess such a thing; the zagmi didn't enforce any rules about the treatment of birds. Still, it seemed like a prize to be gained by inauspicious means, nor did the peddler challenge her notion.

Upon hearing her request, he stepped back from Ziz, also looking left and right to see if they'd been overheard. "What do you want with it?" he asked.

"It's for a friend."

"What does he want with it?"

In that moment, Ziz decided to be honest. The more lies she told, the more difficult they were to sustain, like a book with too many chapters. She was unsure what a lie would even sound like in this context, relative to the truth.

"He'll probably eat it."

The peddler stared at her. What could he possibly have thought?

After a moment, he ducked inside the potter's studio and returned bearing a white feather. Ziz was surprised by how lovely it was. She felt clumsy in its presence. She caught herself holding her breath.

"I don't know if it's real," the peddler admitted. He held the feather while rubbing his neck. There was a tired quality to his voice. "It's the only reason I'll part with it. A person can do amazing things with a tailfeather—do you know that? But I can't make it work."

Rather than answer his question, Ziz imagined the sensation of flying, how the feather could bend and manipulate the air—what it must feel like to be held aloft, like a lasting embrace. To be a bird so white, she'd vanish into the sky and never set foot on solid earth again.

"What will you give me in return?"

This question she did hear. Ziz had anticipated that, if she'd found the thing she was looking for, there would be a steep price to pay. Hazi's credit would do her no good; the peddler didn't spend enough time in Nippur to benefit from it. Ziz had no actual money. Any material possessions she had acquired, she'd already given to Wasu. There was only one thing with which to barter.

"This," she said, reaching into the folds of her dress and removing Meshara's finger.

Ziz had learned of her mother's ceremony not from Meshara, not from Hazi, but from rumors that circulated in the compound. The laundry slaves gossiped to the kitchen slaves when a stain required their ministrations. It seemed that Meshara had acquired her freedom from Temen with an act of self-mutilation. According to the kitchen slaves, the High Zagmi had given his permission.

Ziz had been aghast. What if Temen was still alive somewhere and trying to find his way home? What would he discover upon his arrival—that his wife had been emancipated and his daughter married? Surely, he'd kill Meshara. Perhaps he'd kill them both.

So, she'd taken her mother's finger, as much to spite her as anything else. Ziz was lucky that Meshara hadn't buried it somewhere. Instead, she'd kept it in her sleeping quarters, preserved in an urn full of salt. Ziz doubted that Meshara would notice the finger's absence, though she'd flirted with the idea of smashing the urn, its jagged shards rising from the coarse, white flakes.

"What is it?" the peddler asked.

Ziz held her mother's digit in her open palm, its skin taut and brown. "It's a finger," she said.

"That much is obvious. Whose?"

She'd anticipated this question, too. "With this," Ziz explained, having practiced the words beforehand, "a woman bought her freedom."

There was more to add—she'd carefully rehearsed. What value did freedom have? Freedom could mean nothing to a person born into it, who'd never been promised as a wife or made a slave. To Meshara, it had been worth her fingertip, perhaps more. Perhaps she would've given an arm or a leg, or even both. Despite herself, Ziz admired her mother.

She opened her mouth to expound, but the peddler cut her off. "I'll take it," he said, snatching the offering from Ziz's palm and replacing it with the feather. A totem for a totem.

Now she stood outside Wasu's room, holding the tailfeather aloft. Just the sight of it made Ziz ache. It was the length of her hand, from the base of her palm to the tip of her longest finger, and impossibly light. What she understood about its power, which the peddler had alluded to, stemmed from the stories she'd heard from Temen and Meshara; although, like all of their stories, theirs had differed in the telling.

Meshara had always stressed the feather's capacity to free a person—freedom from gravity, freedom from form. In her stories, crows were shapeshifters, able to enter and exit the netherworld in a variety of guises. However, in Temen's stories, the tailfeather always brought hardship with it, to be used against the crow. Deprived of their tailfeathers, his birds were forced into servitude.

Would Ziz be able to feel its power if it was real? She'd already entertained the notion of keeping it for herself, but how to make it work? The peddler had admitted he couldn't do so. What did Ziz know about magic?

She was jarred from these thoughts when Wasu opened his bedroom door. Ziz couldn't recall another instance of this happening; she'd never seen Wasu anywhere but slouched upon his bed. Now, he leaned against the doorframe, seemingly drained from the effort.

"What did you bring me?" he asked.

She expected the words to elicit a thrill—it had been so long since he'd spoken them. Instead, Ziz hid the tailfeather behind her back. This act of concealment was unnecessary—already Wasu had turned and begun the slow shuffle toward his mattress. He walked heavily, favoring his right leg, and wheezed from the effort. For the first time, Ziz was aware of his height; his girth normally made him appear lower to the ground. If not for whatever ailment afflicted him, Wasu would've been well on his way to manhood. After a moment's hesitation, she followed him inside.

"I got something from a peddler," she said, unhappy to volunteer this information but knowing he could sense a lie.

The obese boy collapsed on his bed. "What?"

Ziz spun the tailfeather on its quill. Reluctantly, she held it where he could see. Wasu squinted.

"Bring it closer."

Her stomach clenched, almost like she was going to vomit. Instead of issuing forth food and bile, words emerged in a rush.

"Remember what you said about the netherworld? About crows? Well...what if they could bring you someplace else? What if I could go back home—

before all of this happened. Do you think that's possible?"

Wasu's mouth opened slightly. He reached out with a soft hand, fingers waggling, making divots in the flesh where his knuckles had disappeared.

"Wasu?"

"I don't know," he muttered, addressing his words to the tailfeather. "Maybe. Let me see."

"Are you going to eat it?"

As he met Ziz's eye, she could see these words have a corrosive effect. Again, Ziz observed the man lurking inside the child—more than his physical bearing, a sense of entitlement, like this impediment to his will was an affront.

"It's for me, isn't it?"

What else could she do? It was his room in his house. Even she belonged to him, in a manner of speaking—a ward with no prospects of her own. Perhaps, if she were kind to him, he would appreciate the gesture; he would appreciate her. Ziz handed him the tailfeather. Wasu snatched it away.

"I don't think it'll work if you eat it," she said—a final bluff.

"How do you know?"

"I don't. I just—"

Wasu tilted back his head and opened his mouth. With one eye, he watched as Ziz squirmed, unable to contain herself, though she knew she was being manipulated. Internally, she chaffed at surrendering so easily. At the same time, she felt powerless to act. It was the same experience as standing before her father and learning her fate.

It was then that Hazi and Meshara entered the room. The children were both surprised. Wasu lowered his chin. Ziz took two steps back from the mattress, her eyes going immediately to Meshara's right hand.

"Here they are," Hazi stated. "Why so quiet? Are we interrupting?"

Wasu swallowed—thankfully, nothing but air.

"No, mother," he said. "We were just ..."

His eyes sought Ziz. She stared back at him.

After a silence, Hazi sighed. "Children and their secrets," she said, ostensibly to Meshara, though Ziz's mother stood her distance, hands clasped before her. "Whatever it was," Hazi continued, "this won't take very long—there's planning to attend to. Wasu, you're getting married."

Ziz witnessed his expression change. Initially, it was one of fear—a sense, in his mother's presence, that he was somehow at fault. This Ziz could see in his downturned lips. That fear didn't leave him, but it was soon tempered by confusion, represented by a frown.

An arranged marriage—Ziz wondered how the notion would affect Wasu, who might've otherwise assumed his autonomy. Did he think it was a choice being presented to him, among the countless other choices he could make on a given day?

"Married?"

"Yes," Hazi confirmed. She no longer smiled. Glancing at Ziz, she added, "To her. Didn't she tell you?"

18

CROW

ONLY A MITU COULD BE SO foolish.

The farmers had dealt with Temen swiftly and severely. The three men were brothers; that much the crow had inferred from listening to them. Even before the sun had set, they'd erected a crucifix from the stiles of the ladder to which they'd bound the mitu. Lacking nails, they'd used pieces of rope to lash his arms, legs, and torso to the wood. They'd also loaned him a pair of their clothes. He was currently wearing the second brother's dress and the youngest brother's hat, its wide brim pulled down. Not so low, however, that he could ignore the crow.

The bird was balanced on Temen's arm, halfway between his elbow and shoulder. It didn't speak—it didn't have to. The comfort of its perch signified everything it might've said about the mitu's naiveté.

"A scarecrow," Temen muttered. "They turned me into a scarecrow."

That word had always been insulting. As if a bundle of sticks and fabric could scare a crow. What did a crow have to fear when it could travel freely between the natural world and the netherworld? Not death. Certainly not this affront.

"MINE," the crow said.

"What? Oh—that."

Yes, the crow thought, that. How to extract its tailfeather from Temen's belly? The bird imagined one of the farmers gutting him with a knife. They didn't seem to be overly concerned about the mitu's well-being, but they hadn't been willing to communicate with the bird, either, shooing the crow away when it had approached them. Maybe another animal would be attracted to the rotting corpse? The crow could appeal to a scavenger—persuade it to do the job with claws and teeth.

"It's too bad," Temen said. "I was going to give it back."

The crow didn't believe him. At the same time, even the possibility was like an unsettling sound. Once heard, it couldn't be unheard. The bird paced the length of Temen's arm, closer to his face.

The mitu smiled. Under the broad brim of the farmer's hat, his teeth flashed against his dark-hued lips.

"Stop it," he said. "That tickles."

Something about his jocularity incensed the crow. It advanced even closer—close enough peck at his cheek. The mitu was unable to turn away or even to defend himself, but neither did he seem to mind the crow's assault. It promptly made a hole in his skin, rapping its beak against the enamel of his teeth.

Temen laughed.

"That doesn't even hurt, you stupid bird."

The crow knew it was true—the mitu couldn't feel pain. At that very moment, though his internal organs sagged under the weight of gravity, Temen remained content. His joints were being taxed, but he'd remain blissfully unaware until his shoulders were pulled from their sockets and his lungs collapsed. The crow stopped pecking. The mitu's cheek was in tatters. He gazed at the bird with his good eye, not bothering to turn his face.

"Get me down from here."

What choice did it have? Whether the crow capitulated now or later, the result would be the same—and maybe, if it acquiesced more quickly, the mitu would return its tailfeather as promised. Maybe he was telling the truth.

The crow didn't believe this, but pretending felt slightly better.

The farmers had bound Temen by the wrists. The bird decided to begin with his right hand so the mitu could aid with the effort. The rope was loose, which made it easy to tease without also pecking the man, but it was slow to unravel. The light dimmed as the crow worked. The mitu didn't offer encouragement, and, after a while, the bird imagined it was performing an act of vandalism, dismantling an actual scarecrow under the cover of darkness. Its kind had been known to do this, though it was far easier and less time-consuming to just ignore the scarecrow, once identified as such.

Finally, it had caused enough duress to the rope so Temen could free his hand. The crow immediately abandoned its perch. It was a long way to the ground. The bird landed on its side.

"Turned me into a scarecrow," Temen muttered again. There was a darkness to his voice that made the crow wary. Still, it thought to caution him as he tugged at the rope around his chest.

"NO."

"No?" Temen snapped. "Why not?"

But there was neither time nor the requisite number of syllables to explain. As soon as Temen had released his torso, gravity claimed the bulk of his body—gravity, as the crow knew, being the greatest scavenger of all. Temen was left hanging by his wrist. He swung lazily, to and fro. The crucifix whined and bent. The stiles themselves were not thick, given their original purpose, but the farmers had planted them deep in the ground to prevent the apparatus from tipping.

Temen reached for his wrist with his free hand. "You." He snarled. It was unclear whether he was blaming the bird, asking it for help, or both.

The crow deliberated. If it perched on the depressed end of the crucifix, would its weight cause the structure to tip? Between its feathers and its hollow bones, it didn't possess much heft. Conversely, it would be no small effort to ascend Temen's body. What previously would've required little thought now involved an awkward combination of flapping and clawing, like some hybrid beast that boasted the worst combination of bits and pieces.

"Do something," the mitu insisted.

Again, gravity acted before the crow was required to. With a rip and a pop, Temen's arm separated from his body. Normally a shoulder would dislocate without incident, but the mitu's flesh lacked the resiliency of a living person. It shredded like burlap.

Temen fell to the ground, not unlike the crow a moment before, landing in a disconsolate heap. His severed limb remained tied to the stile, its fingers wagging.

The crow had the good sense to back away. Somehow, it knew, it would be blamed for this development. In fact, it was inspired to find another scapegoat, and soon—somewhere else to direct Temen's rage, in order to be spared that ordeal.

"THEY," the crow cawed.

Temen moaned. He didn't right himself. The absence of his arm had yet to be addressed.

"MADE," the crow continued, seizing upon the mitu's previous condemnation that the farmers had turned him into a scarecrow. And why not? The crow was familiar with these feelings. The farmers had overpowered Temen. They'd ignored his protests, as well as his pleas.

They'd turned him into something he didn't recognize—used his body to suit their needs. The presence of a mitu would be more off-putting than a normal scarecrow, his flesh repugnant. Temen had become a thing, like a bridle or a yoke. He hated the farmers. He also hated himself. This deeper, more personal hatred would sustain the other.

"YOU."

Temen sat up. It seemed difficult to do so with only one arm—his balance had been impaired. He looked around himself, ultimately focusing his attention on the crucifix and not the crow.

"SCARE—"

"No."

He said it gently, sounding more confused than alarmed. But staring at his severed limb, its fingers like worms after a hard rain, a note of alarm and—yes—disgust had entered his voice.

"CROW."

"No."

Temen turned. How fast could he move, were he inclined to strike? Not very, from his seated position, especially given his challenged equilibrium. He'd catch the crow eventually, so the bird struggled to add more. 'Farmers' would take too long, as would 'brothers.'

"Where did they go?" Temen snarled.

The farmers' dwelling was on the other side of the orchard; they'd left after completing their work, walking in a direction that Temen couldn't see. He now seemed content to follow the crow, as soon as his other arm had been untied. The bird tried not to gawk as Temen carried his limb balanced against his shoulder. The severed elbow bent at his neck, curving over his back in a kind of embrace, while the fingers reached for anything to grasp. Temen held it firmly by the wrist, palm angled outward. Behind him, the crucifix pitched in the moonlight.

The crow couldn't guess what he intended to do. There were three farmers. Any retribution Temen had planned would surely wake one of them before he could subdue the others, and even the youngest farmer presented a challenge for a man with only one arm.

When they came to the dwelling, the crow spotted the thing that Temen had originally requested.

"MULE."

The pathetic animal was asleep on its feet, tied to a stake, but the mitu showed little interest. He walked right past the mule, toward the dwelling, and idled in the doorway.

Outside, a pile of ladders and baskets lay on one side, the tools required to maintain an orchard. On the other side was an empty pen. The crow recognized a glow that emanated from inside the dwelling. The farmers slept with their cookfire still burning.

"GO," the crow cawed as quietly as it was able. Temen had escaped his confinement. Unlike the crow, he was able to leave. The bird was concerned that, if the mitu awoke the slumbering farmers, they'd enact some terrible violence upon him and render its tailfeather inaccessible, either because he'd been burned, buried, or worse.

"GO. NOW."

Temen lowered the arm from his shoulder. He still held it by the wrist, but now the severed hand could clasp his forearm in return, like a fraternal greeting. Wielding the limb this way, he stepped inside. The crow hopped after him.

The three farmers were arranged around the fire. The youngest one lay nearest the door. The crow didn't trust itself to speak without waking them, so it watched in silence as Temen knelt beside the sleeping youth.

"Hey."

He placed the severed arm on the farmer's chest. The hand swept left and right, its fingers plucking at the boy's sleep garment and prodding his ribs. Then, laboriously, it began to crawl up the young man's chest.

"Hey," Temen said, keeping his voice low. "Wake up, you."

The crow nervously flapped its wings as the farmer stirred. He opened his eyes at roughly the same instant that the hand reached his throat.

His lips parted, but he couldn't speak—the hand had a stranglehold, as if Temen were sharing his most intimate desires. Or not. Perhaps, the crow thought, the hand possessed its own murderous intent, an even more distressing thought.

"I got down," Temen said, stating the obvious." I'm going to take a mule now. But I wanted to leave you with this."

As he said it, he rose to full height. Perhaps the farmer had been staring at the mitu's face as he spoke—perhaps he'd assumed Temen's arm was still connected. But now, as Temen backed away, a look of terror distorted the boy's features. He wheezed and hissed, his eyes bulging, as he desperately tried to remove the hand from his throat. Through it all, the other brothers slept. The crow heard the sound of the farmer's larynx being crushed. It watched the severed arm sway like a serpent's tail.

"Come on," Temen said. He must've anticipated the bird's query, because he added, "It'll do them, next. After that, I don't know. Let's not find out."

19

MESHARA

MESHARA MARVELED at how quickly things had changed.

Ziz was engaged to Hazi's younger son. It was unclear whether this had been Temen and Garash's original intent, or if, like Ziz said, she'd been promised to a soldier. It didn't matter—none of the men were present to voice an opinion. In their absence, Hazi had arranged matters as she saw fit.

Gone was Meshara's plan to flee Nippur. It seemed safer and more natural to accommodate Hazi's wishes, especially if this marriage meant greater security for herself—though, really, what difference would it make if Ziz's actions came to light? Would the death of Garash now be considered patricide? Would the punishment be even worse? Or would Ziz's newfound status spare her? From what

Meshara could see, rich people often did terrible things without fear of retribution. They wrote their own rules.

Anyhow, there could be no slipping away—not with a wedding to organize.

Here, for perhaps the first time, Meshara's sense of protocol outweighed Hazi's. Of course, the other woman would be in charge of the invitations, as it was she who'd be hosting the event. Not to mention that Meshara didn't know a single person in Nippur. How was it possible she'd spent all this time in the city, only to know Hazi?

It was because Hazi had claimed her, a dynamic she suspected would only deepen now that their children were to be wed. First, she'd belonged to Temen, and now she belonged to her matron.

"We'll be sisters," Hazi said as they strolled back from the bazaar. It wasn't the first time she'd said it —she seemed to be in love with the words.

"Not exactly," Meshara disagreed, also not for the first time. "That's not how it works."

"What does it matter? We are what we say. Do you want the High Zagmi to make it official? He can say something at the ceremony. I'm sure he'll repeat whatever I tell him."

Meshara was carrying all the items they'd purchased, walking a step or two behind Hazi. For the wedding ceremony, Meshara had insisted on making a traditional goat stew. Hazi had demurred, but, on this matter, Meshara would not be swayed. Goat stew had been served at her wedding, at her mother's wedding, and at countless weddings before them. It didn't matter whether she slaughtered the goat herself. Hazi could cater the rest of the event as she saw fit, so long as Meshara got her way.

The alleyways were crowded. People parted for Hazi like a river around a boulder while Meshara turned her shoulders sideways to knife a path.

"Have you heard men call each other brother?" Hazi asked. "I have sons—they're brothers. No two people could be more different. Do you think Garash and your husband think of each other this way? How funny that they know each other. Or knew—I forget I'm speaking to a free woman."

This last comment she delivered with a smirk. Meshara attempted to smile, if only to mask her discomfort. Did Hazi mean to mock her? Was she able to derive confidence from another person's shame? Meshara didn't know for whom she smiled, but already, the rich woman had turned away.

The kitchen was bustling with activity when they entered from the street. Per Hazi's order, a small area had been cleared for Meshara's food preparation, and it was here that she unloaded her parcel—onion, garlic, ginger, carrots, and potatoes. Five slaves were vying for space, two more than usual, as they produced finger foods and took receipt of various ales. Wasu and Ziz were to be married the next day. Because they were so young, Hazi had observed, they didn't require a long engagement, nor would they live on their own for some time. To Meshara's mind, this had meant the ceremony could wait, but Hazi was determined. Perhaps she sensed Ziz's reticence, Meshara thought, evident when she stood in Wasu's presence, or maybe Hazi acted out of boredom.

"The goat will be delivered this afternoon," Hazi said, lifting a stewed date from a nearby platter. "I asked the butcher if you could kill it yourself. Not really—but you would, wouldn't you? You have before?"

Again, Meshara forced a smile. "How else would we eat?"

"Of course. It's just so…grim."

The cook was standing close enough to overhear, wearing her customary scowl. She snorted at this last comment, though it was clear she meant no disrespect toward Hazi. Feeling provoked by the other woman's presence, Meshara smiled sweetly at her matron.

"When we're sisters," she said, "I'll show you how to slaughter a goat. There are so many things we'll be able to do—places to go and secrets to keep. I've never had a sister before. Do you still plan on growing your hair?"

Hazi absently raised a hand to her head.

"Yes?"

"Then I will, too. People will say we're twins."

Hazi laughed uncomfortably at this. It was the first time Meshara had seen her flustered. Was it the suggestion of intimacy? Or the threat of blood?

"Twins are bad luck," Hazi observed as she backed out of the kitchen. "They'd have to drown one of us in a well, and it wouldn't be me! Go and make your stew. Come find me when you're done, and we'll discuss what to wear."

With that, she left. A feeling of relief passed over the kitchen, like a calm through a herd. None of the slaves raised her eyes from her task, but now they looked down because it was prudent to do so, not to avoid their matron's gaze.

Meshara inspected the vegetables before her. Prior to chopping them, she had decided to gather her spices, cumin and thyme. She'd forgotten to buy parsley, but she assumed she could borrow some from another workstation.

As she went to the pantry, her thoughts turned to the meat about to be delivered. How well did Hazi know the butcher? Presumably, he'd been hired on a recommendation. But what did that say about his proficiency? Had he castrated the goat right after the slaughter? For how long had he aged the carcass?

And what cut would he provide for the stew, the neck or the shoulder?

It saddened Meshara that Ziz wouldn't know to ask these questions. What use would she have for them, coming of age in Hazi's compound? Meshara could offer her instruction, but how would she truly learn if she never applied the lessons? More likely, Ziz would become adept at cultivating relationships with people like the High Zagmi. She'd gain these skills by watching, if she weren't explicitly taught, just as Meshara had learned the intricacies of turning a crop from watching her father-in-law.

Ziz would lead a different life. And if she someday had a daughter, and that young woman was promised in marriage, Meshara would prepare a goat stew for her—or not, if she were already dead. Food would still be eaten. No one would go hungry.

Meshara returned to her workstation with her spices cupped in each hand. She hadn't wanted to carry the containers, lest she deprive another cook of the same thing. When she got there, a curious sight awaited her; her station, or what she believed to be her station, had been cleaned. Gone were her purchased food items. Gone was the knife she'd laid aside for herself. All that remained was the copper pot she'd chosen earlier that day. If not for its presence, she might've thought she was lost.

Carefully, she tipped her spices into two piles,

cleaning her palms against the sides of her dress. Whatever mistake had been made was easily corrected. Meshara would either locate the missing ingredients or replace them with no time lost. Was it possible the meat had been delivered in her absence? No, she thought, she hadn't been gone that long.

Turning to address the nearest slave, she found herself facing the cook. The woman had approached without making a sound—and now Meshara gleaned the true nature of this conflict.

The two women stared at each other. Meshara was a head taller, but the cook was stouter. Her jaw was clenched. After a moment, it became apparent she wouldn't speak first, so Meshara initiated the debate.

"My things," Meshara said. "Where can I find them?"

"Someone else will make the stew. You can go."

"It's my stew—I'll make it myself."

Just as before, a feeling took hold of the room, a mood of anxious waiting. If the kitchen slaves really had been a herd, their noses would've been raised and their ears perked.

The cook flared her nostrils. She took a step toward Meshara, violating an invisible boundary. She would never stand this close to Hazi—none of the slaves would.

"You," the woman sneered. "Who are you? You

and your evil daughter. You think I don't know? Only rarely does she try to conceal it—nuts, fruit, bread. At the bazaar, she's called a thief. They say she blinded a man, that the matron had to make amends. I ask you, what woman raises such a child? Or maybe she raises herself? While you're busy following the matron around—always at her heel, like some kind of dog."

Meshara had backed away from this litany. She could feel the blood rising to her cheeks. As far as she knew, everything the cook had said was accurate—about Hazi, about Ziz, about the bazaar. Still, she knew she had to contest it. Otherwise, the slight would become a matter of lore and no subsequent effort could change it.

All she managed to say was, "You can't—"

"Go," the cook curtailed her thought. "Out of my kitchen! Whatever you are—dog, whore—I am in charge here. I am the matron—me. Even the master knows it, when he returns. He stands over there, by the door, and asks, 'What smells so good?' He asks what he can eat, unlike your evil daughter, who takes what she pleases. I will slap the master's hand if he gets too greedy. Ask anyone. This kitchen belongs to me."

All the other slaves had paused in their labors to stare at the two women. Meshara held her breath. To release it would mean breathing in the cook's face.

Instead, she turned, having nowhere else to go, and faced her desolate workstation.

"Stew." The cook spat the word. "I'll make your stew. What could be easier? And when your daughter marries that monster—"

Meshara swung the copper pot by its handle. It connected with the cook's brow, making a gonging noise, but it only appeared to stun the other woman, who staggered backward.

Using both hands, Meshara swung the pot again, this time in a chopping motion from high to low. She struck the cook on the bridge of the nose. Blood spurted everywhere, as the other woman collapsed to the floor.

Meshara continued to bludgeon her. When the cook shielded her head, Meshara aimed for her back. When her contortions exposed her head again, Meshara swung there. The pot was beginning to lose its shape.

If Meshara had any thoughts at all, it was the implication that she was somehow less than a slave—the audacity of that notion. She was a free woman. Her daughter had been promised to the son of a wealthy landowner. In no room of this house, or any other house, was she less than this person—this *thing*. To allow that kind of thinking would allow anyone to disrespect her.

Finally, her arms tired. The cook had long since

ceased to move. Meshara discarded the pot—now shaped like a butterfly net, it clanged to the floor. Her chest heaved as she stood over the body. When she straightened her spine, her eyes met those of the other kitchen slaves, uniformly wide with fear.

This kitchen belongs to me.

"Carrots," Meshara said.

There was no motion at first. The room remained frozen.

"Carrots," she repeated.

A young slave, perhaps a year or two older than Ziz, retrieved her carrots from where they'd been hidden and delivered them to her workstation.

"Onion," Meshara demanded. "Garlic. Ginger. Potatoes."

She stood, imperious, as these items were also returned to her one by one, along with the knife she'd chosen and a new pot to cook in. Every slave partook in this exercise—no one wanted to be seen as defiant. When they were done, Meshara knew they would also remove the cook's body. She wouldn't have to instruct them to do so—Meshara's desires would flow like a spring thaw from the peaks of Mashu.

When the butcher came, she'd confront him, too—maybe even send him back for another cut of meat. It was her kitchen now.

20

ZIZ

As a result of their engagement, Wasu was a changed man.

At least that was how he was perceived, if not by Ziz, then by the rest of the household—as a man, now. A new master to obey. Slaves attended to his needs with alacrity, showing greater care with the clothes he wore and the frequency with which he was bathed. Of course, his mother still presided over any major decision, but Wasu's agency could be observed in how he treated the people in his sway—most notably, Ziz.

Now *he* presented *her* with gifts. Ziz didn't know where he acquired these items, fabrics and jewelry, often paired to aesthetic effect. None of it, she thought, was really meant to appeal to her. Since when had she demonstrated an interest in dressing like a rich woman? When he gave her these things, most likely acquired from his mother's wardrobe, it was to outfit Ziz as Wasu would prefer to see her.

The most important gift would be the bridal present. In her head, Ziz harbored a secret hope that Wasu would return the tailfeather—not only that he'd acknowledge how much it had meant to her, but that he'd be willing to part with it, too, actually providing her with something she wanted.

She felt certain he hadn't eaten it, but only because she couldn't countenance the idea. There was magic in the tailfeather. Somehow, it could change the situation in which she'd found herself—all her freedoms forfeit, all her desires proscribed.

Thankfully, the gifting of the bridal present didn't require its own ceremony. On the day that Wasu gave it to her, Ziz had been testing pillows for their future bedroom. She'd never slept on a pillow before. Now, she obediently raised and lowered her head as slaves substituted one pillow after another, asking her to note their relative firmness. So this was what opulence felt like—drooling on a cloud.

She looked up at their expectant faces, arranged in a circle above her. "Yes," she said. "Good. The best one so far."

Wasu entered the room on the arm of a slave. As part of his transformation, he'd become increasingly ambulatory, though he still required help and grew tired easily. His presence was immediately noted—all the other slaves vacated the room, taking the pillows with them and leaving Ziz splayed on the floor. Wasu's aid also left after a stool had been fetched and Wasu's comfort assured.

"So," he said, his reedy voice echoing in the empty room. "Pillows?"

"Yes, pillows."

He nodded judiciously, as though she'd provided a great insight. "Any good ones?"

"Some."

Ziz continued to lay on the sleeping mat, her hands folded over her belly. Should she have stood in Wasu's presence? She didn't know the proper protocol.

"What did you bring for me?" she said.

If he understood the joke, he didn't acknowledge it. Instead, Wasu reached between the folds of his dress. Ziz's heart rose and fell as, predictably, he removed an object that wasn't the tailfeather. He'd never give it back, she knew. This certainty was like a stone lodged in her gut. The feather represented freedom, unlike his clothes and jewels, all of which served to remind her of her place. That didn't stop her from wishing, no matter how ludicrous. Brief moments such as this, when her spirits were buoyed, had become the cause of simmering resentment.

When she did see what he was holding, her stomach clenched.

"It makes an engraving," Wasu said, holding the cylinder aloft. "What you do—"

"I know what it is."

"What you do," Wasu repeated himself, frowning at her interruption, "is roll it over clay. This one shows the gods on parade. I'll have a slave bring us some clay—I wanted to show you first."

Ziz sat up and reached for the cylinder. She remembered how it felt, its heft and polished smoothness. She even remembered what the first one had looked like as it had spun, end over end, into the ravine.

"It's your bridal gift."

Wasu maintained his grip even as she closed her palm around it. Was she not supposed to touch it?

Ziz tugged on the cylinder. When she did so, Wasu came tumbling off his stool like a fleshy avalanche. First his knees touched the ground, eliciting a wince, and still, he fell. Ziz scampered backwards, but it was no use—the obese boy collapsed upon her.

His weight was smothering, like being trapped under a heavy blanket. It was also malleable. Rather than press down, his flesh shaped itself around her contours. She couldn't dig in her heels. She had one hand with which to leverage herself, the other still clasped around the cylinder.

Ziz didn't understand. Had this been Wasu's intent? Was he exerting himself or in a state of distress? Either way, it seemed paramount to call for help—for him, for her, or at least to summon a witness. But how could she call out when her voice was trapped inside her chest? Her mouth was like a cave from which no breath could escape. Now that he was down from the stool, Wasu had released the bridal gift. He hugged his arms around Ziz's thighs. She watched in horror as he began to kiss her knees, the fabric of her dress turning dark with spit.

The cylinder was still in her hand, as substantial as the tailfeather had been light. *What did you bring me?* Wasu had brought her a weapon.

Ziz imagined what it would feel like to swing for his head, and then she did the very thing.

Immediately, she knew the damage she'd wrought. Wasu grunted. She struck him again on very nearly the same place, and he rolled to one side, allowing her to scurry away.

"Help!" he said.

How different would it have been had Ziz called for help instead? Would the slaves have heard her? What might they have done, hearing a female call for assistance, rather than a male? Would they have been as responsive? Or would they have looked into each other's eyes, waiting to see who reacted first, a permission of sorts?

Regardless, it *wasn't* Ziz who'd called for help. The word was still caught in her throat, having traveled that far and no farther.

The first slaves through the door looked aghast. They helped Wasu onto his stool, straining their postures as they lifted him. Already Ziz could see a welt forming on his forehead. She was pleased for the evidence of her defense, even if it could be used against her. Looking down, she also confirmed the blotches of saliva on her dress, further confirmation of what had occurred. And, of course, there was the bridal gift in her hand. Ziz kept a firm grip, lest she be forced to use it again.

"She hit me," Wasu complained. Ziz wondered to whom he was addressing himself—the slaves? They dared not respond. It was hardly their place to say whether this represented appropriate behavior.

"You kissed me," she retorted.

Wasu's cheeks became as red as his welt. "You're my wife," he insisted. "I can do as I please."

"I'm not your wife yet."

"But you were promised to me!"

Ziz looked down at her bridal gift. After all, that's what it represented—her fealty to Wasu. One man, presumably dead, had made a promise to a second man, also dead. As a result, she now belonged to a third man.

No matter that it could be used as a weapon or that it had spared her from Wasu's advances, if only for a moment. The cylinder was their contract.

"I don't want to be."

With these words, she hurled the cylinder—a second time, she couldn't help but think. She aimed for the far wall. Having already injured Wasu once, it seemed imprudent to do so again. Did Ziz imagine the stone breaking upon contact, as if to symbolize her intent?

It didn't, of course. It did, however, put a dent in the mud-brick carpentry, a story for future slaves to embellish among themselves.

A good number of slaves were already in attendance. Presumably, one had run for Hazi at the first sign of distress, because now the matron entered the room.

Her timing was fortuitous—she was there to see the cylinder hit the wall. Meshara saw, too. As always, she stood at her matron's heel, but now her expression was aghast, whereas normally she was the picture of complicity.

"Ziz!"

"I don't want to. Let's go—let's leave, like you said."

"What do you mean 'leave'?" Wasu said.

"I mean what I mean. My mother's a free woman and so am I."

She didn't know if this last part was true, only that it should've been. Must the High Zagmi emancipate her, too? But emancipate her from what? She wasn't actually married yet—she hadn't entered into a contract. What did it matter what Temen had said if she was unwilling to participate? Couldn't she make these decisions for herself?

Wasu seemed genuinely bereft. "You'd go?" he asked her. "You wouldn't be my wife?"

Ziz looked down at her dress. All the stains had faded except for one, which retained the shape of Wasu's lips, pursed and wet. She tried to imagine a lifetime of those lips pressing against her mouth, her cheek, her neck. She imagined him endlessly spilling off his stool, like a permanently tumbling mass, crushing her under his weight. She stopped her suppositions at the thought of children—boys like Wasu, with absolute power, and girls like herself, forced to comply.

"No," she said, shuddering with revulsion. "I belong to myself."

Hazi snorted. When she opened her mouth to speak, Wasu preceded her.

"She killed my father! She killed Garash!"

Ziz's jaw dropped. Everything changed at once.

Wasu sneered. "You think I don't know? He talks

to me. He doesn't know he's dead—or he knows but he can't remember. He's someplace else, all alone. He looks like he did when he was young."

The obese boy turned to his mother, who looked the way Ziz felt, devoid of thought. Was she surprised by what he'd said? Wasu was different—everyone knew this. Why not believe he could see the dead?

"She killed father," Wasu insisted, reaching for Hazi's hand. "She—it's hard for me to say. He looks different now, but something bit him—something big, right on the neck. She tricked him. Father's dead, and it's all because of her."

He attempted to collect his mother's hands, but she shook him off—absently, at first, but with increasing conviction.

"No," Hazi murmured. "No." Like an incantation, the word gained volume with every repetition. "No." A plea. "No!" A denial of Wasu, but also of what he was saying. From a place deep within her. Even as she rejected her husband's death, Hazi mourned for him. "NO!" She keened. "NO! NO!"

Her face formed a hideous expression. For the first time that day, Ziz felt truly afraid—a feeling that began in her gut and seeped down to her limbs. Even in the bazaar, when she'd blinded the man, she hadn't been so scared.

Before her stood Hazi. Behind Hazi stood

Meshara, and to either side of her was a motionless slave, none of them sympathetic. And there was Wasu—fat, simpering Wasu, to whom she never should've revealed herself.

Hazi lunged at her. Had they really been so close that it could happen so fast? If Wasu had been an avalanche, his mother was a wave.

She knocked Ziz off her feet and pinned her to the floor. Ziz could count the teeth in Hazi's head. She could feel her nails digging into her wrists, and though she tried to free herself, the rich woman was fierce with sorrow. She was drooling.

It was Meshara who finally separated them, pulling Hazi off. Not that it mattered. Now or later, Ziz would meet a violent end—this much had become clear. She'd upset the natural order of things. Recompense was due and she had no way to pay.

Hazi continued to struggle. She hurled herself at Meshara while staring at Ziz, raging, yelling loud enough to bring down the walls.

"YOU WILL DIE! YOU WILL DIE!"

21

CROW

TEMEN RODE through the night and into the following day. They were going back to his dwelling. He'd announced this only once, after orienting himself against Mashu, and had then imposed silence.

The march was dreary. Temen didn't require food or water, or even intermittent breaks to relieve himself. For the purpose of their journey, he allowed the crow to perch on the bridle, so long as it stayed off his head and shoulders. He had no further use for the bird, but seemed accustomed to its company, while the crow still harbored a hope of reclaiming its tailfeather.

The mule, for its part, was also silent. Some animals were like that—taciturn. It was especially common among domesticated beasts, whether it was because they'd lost the facility for speaking or because their servitude had left them feeling alienated.

At one point, Temen asked, "How long has it been?" He could've meant anything—how long it had been since he'd murdered the farmer, how long had it been since he'd stolen the tailfeather. The crow remained silent.

"My landlord was supposed to visit," he continued. His voice sounded coarse. Ever since losing an arm, his body had begun to deteriorate more swiftly, such that the smell would soon attract carrion birds. "My daughter is promised to his son. How long since we traveled to the netherworld?"

The crow couldn't provide an accurate answer. Time passed more slowly in the netherworld than it did in the natural world, even though the sun rose there when it set here and vice versa.

"WEEKS."

The mitu winced, an ugly sight. "Maybe he's already been," he said. "My wife will please him—she'll make him feel welcome. But my daughter, she hasn't learned her place yet…"

Temen's voice trailed off. The crow didn't care. There was nothing to be learned from this dialogue. A greater number of humans at the dwelling meant a greater likelihood of violence. Or, perhaps, if Temen were restored to his previous life—with his wife, child, and landlord—he would be more inclined to give back the crow's tailfeather. The bird clung to this belief, for lack of anything else to sustain it.

They were lucky not to encounter other people. Maybe word of the mitu had preceded them. Maybe they were being watched even now, as they trudged by various indicators of human habitation, like rows of crops and irrigation canals.

Temen didn't make an effort to avoid detection. If he'd learned anything from his run-in with the farmers, those lessons weren't on public display, though the crow was unable to intuit his private thoughts. And what about those farmers—were they all dead now, strangled by the mitu's disassociated limb? How could he ever be at peace, knowing a part of himself was still at large, a separate entity in this vast and crowded world?

They arrived at the family dwelling at last. For the first time since they'd left the apple orchard, Temen dismounted the mule, tying the animal to a hitching post without bothering to water it. But first, the crow had to jump down from the bridle—a terrifying leap of only a few feet, given its useless wings.

How sad to consider this an act of bravery, or else to think of it as falling. The bird had spent practically its entire life in flight, yet already it had forgotten the sensation. It was as much a slave to gravity as its traveling companions.

"Where is everyone?" Temen observed. He was looking at the fields. From where it stood, the crow could only see Temen's knees, so it remained mute. The mitu turned back toward the dwelling. "They should be working," he said. "There was...salt?"

The crow tried to map what it could see of the farm from its previous perspective—the crops, the garden, and the dwelling, all from above. Temen began to walk and the crow followed.

In front of the dwelling was a wide, brown stain that had once been blood—there was no mistaking it for anything else. The ground was also spattered with bird droppings, as were the walls and roof. The crow guessed a variety of species had made it their roost, and it could see why—the husks of dried grains, scattered high and low, where they'd been randomly distributed. The crow pecked at one such remnant. Even the hint of nourishment made it giddy with relief. It proceeded to gorge itself on the grain like a baby chick, pitiful and gluttonous.

The mitu considered the scene before him—the blood, the grains, the droppings. He turned to stare at the fields again, squinting into the sun, then returned his attention to the dwelling. Meanwhile, the crow pecked at another husk. Its stomach, no bigger than a pebble, grudgingly expanded to fit this bounty. Out of the corner of its eye, it noted when Temen stepped forward, carefully negotiating the blood stain. It didn't see what happened next, only that something flew from the dwelling and struck him on the side of the head, knocking him back a pace.

"Hamta!" the mitu shouted, more in surprise than in pain.

The object appeared to be a ball of dough. Curious, the crow pecked at it, but found that it had long since petrified and was now too hard to penetrate. It returned to its meal of discarded grains.

"Stay away," came a voice from within.

"This is my home," Temen said. "Who are you? Come out."

"Stay away," the voice insisted a second time. Another projectile followed—a clay bowl that narrowly missed Temen, arcing and landing with a thud.

The mitu stood on the far side of the blood stain, considering his options. The crow had eaten all it could after being starved for so long and staggered from one husk to the next as if intoxicated. Its stomach felt deliciously, painfully full, almost to the point of bursting. With this fullness came an attendant dizziness. For once, it was relieved to be so low to the ground.

Finally, Temen said, "I'll burn it down if you don't come out. I'll light everything on fire, with you in it. How about that?"

A long silence elapsed as the person considered the mitu's threat.

"You can come in," the voice relented in an apparent act of compromise.

Temen looked at the crow. "You first."

The crow wasn't afraid, but neither was it stupid; whoever was inside the dwelling wasn't likely to relax upon seeing the mitu and his pet. However, the threat of violence also existed outside the dwelling. At least it had eaten, the crow thought. To die after a meal, no matter how paltry, was better than dying on an empty stomach.

The bird hopped over the blood stain. It couldn't identify the wounded animal from the smell—something big enough to have bled prodigiously.

Inside the dwelling, it took a moment for the crow's eyes to adjust to the light. The cookfire wasn't lit, nor had it been for some time. The shadows were deep. The air was cool. What few possessions Temen and his family had accrued over the years seemed to be piled on the far end of the circular enclosure, like a barricade. Behind that barricade was a boy.

At first, the crow could only see the boy's eyes. Preternaturally white, they appeared to float at the rear of the dwelling. Soon, a face came into focus. The crow could tell at once that he was hungry. Not the mild hunger that came from anticipating a meal

—the deeper pangs of privation. Why hadn't the boy eaten the grains? What prevented him from leaving the dwelling when food was so readily available outside? Perhaps the animal that had created the stain?

The boy was holding another projectile—some kind of cooking implement. Upon seeing the crow, he stood a little taller.

"You're...small," he said.

The crow didn't appreciate this observation. "YOU," it cawed—meaning, the boy was hardly any bigger.

"Are you an Asag?"

It was a curious question, but the crow had no time to answer. Temen had entered the dwelling. The boy cowered. What could he see of the mitu in the dark? His coloration? His missing limb? Whatever he did see, it wasn't equal to Temen's grotesqueness.

"What're you doing here?" Temen demanded. "Where's my wife?"

"You're—" the boy stammered.

"This is my home. Who are you?"

"They're gone. The Asag ate them."

"What?"

"The Asag," the boy whimpered. "Didn't you see the blood? I could hear her walking on the roof. When I woke up, on the first day, and the day after that. Did you see her?"

"There's no such thing as an Asag," Temen snapped, causing the boy to flinch. "When did you arrive? Where's my family?"

"I don't know—I don't know where anybody is. I came with Garash. There was a woman and a girl. When I woke up, everyone was gone. He said—"

The boy's eyes darted to the doorway.

"He said there's a monster called an Asag. He said she lays her eggs in people. I could hear her on the roof."

Temen grunted. The utterance of the other man's name seemed to have resolved some internal concern. He now stepped deeper into the dwelling, apparently unconcerned that the boy might throw things at him, nor did the boy appear to represent a threat. He'd lost what little animation he had, looking hollow-eyed and tired.

"Birds," Temen said, taking a seat by the extinguished cookfire. "That's what you heard. There's grain everywhere—you heard them eating on the roof."

"But the blood—"

"Not from a person. You were fooled. Now go start a fire. There's some wood outside—nothing will eat you."

The mitu made this final observation with a chuckle. To the crow, it was unclear whether he meant to deride the boy or share in the humor, but the child, still staring at the doorway, produced a feeble smile. He continued to hold the cooking implement by his side—a wooden spoon, the crow could see.

"Hamta!" Temen said. "Do something to make yourself useful."

And so the boy did.

The crow hopped out of his way. It recognized the manner in which Temen spoke to him, the pomposity of one in possession of power. Perhaps if the mitu had a new lackey, he would dismiss the crow? After all, here they were, at Temen's dwelling, per his request. There was no reason to withhold the crow's tailfeather any longer.

"I saw Garash in the netherworld," Temen muttered to himself. "Not Meshara or Ziz. Is that how this works? Would I have seen them, too?"

"MINE," the crow cawed, ignoring his question.

"If they're not here, where did they go? They would've been scared. Her parents would hide her—"

"MINE."

"What?" Temen grunted.

"MINE. YOU. MINE."

Temen squinted at the bird. The crow recognized in the mitu a dawning realization just as the boy returned. Temen smiled an ugly smile, more of a sneer, and sat back with his one remaining hand upon his knee.

"Have you ever seen a bird fly without its tail-feather?"

The boy dropped his load of wood beside the cookfire. "It can't," he said, turning to look at the crow. "Right?"

The bird felt a deepening sense of dread. "MINE," it cawed.

"Of course it can. Watch."

The mitu moved swiftly. He expertly negotiated his mass and momentum, transitioning first to one knee and then to his feet, while scooping up the bird by its undercarriage. The crow struggled, but its wings were pinned against its sides. It pecked at Temen's ribcage, knowing full well he couldn't feel it, the piercing of his flesh. Undaunted, the mitu walked to the door.

Temen threw the bird underhand. It didn't travel very far. Where it landed on the ground, a dirt cloud billowed. The crow allowed itself a moment before attempting to rise, blinking and recalling how it had once soared high above the world. From such heights, it wouldn't have been able to distinguish Temen's face. All it would've seen was a pale smudge, of no greater significance than a rock or a tree. From such heights, the mitu would've been harmless, but here on earth, that wasn't the case. On earth, Temen could dictate the bird's life or death. The crow was powerless.

The boy guffawed. Slowly, the crow righted itself and began to hop toward the dwelling.

"Kick it," Temen commanded. The boy glanced at him. "Kick it," he said again.

The youth moved swiftly, inspired by fear, or perhaps his own dormant cruelty. His kick sent the bird even farther than Temen's throw. His punt was hard and true. Bones snapped. This time, before it hit the ground, the crow had resigned itself to die.

* * *

NIGHT HAD FALLEN. The day was done. The crow passed in and out of consciousness. It didn't know how many times. It didn't bother to lift its head.

From this vantage point, it could see a light that originated from within the dwelling. It filled the doorway and puddled on the ground, much like the puddle of blood. Occasionally, the crow could hear voices—mostly Temen, but sometimes the boy. Once, very clearly, it heard to the child ask, "What's wrong with you?"

"Nothing's wrong with me," Temen said. "I'm fine."

The crow envied their rapport. Certainly, it was easier for the boy to communicate with Temen because he could employ multiple syllables at a time. But even if the crow had been more fluent, there was a complicity that existed between the two humans that couldn't be matched by a human and a bird.

The crow assumed they'd leave in the morning and, in doing so, would leave it behind—no longer of use, had it possessed any value to begin with. Perhaps the boy would ride behind the mitu on the mule, skin pressed against skin, with no feathers to divide them.

"Hey."

The crow didn't need to move its head to locate the voice. It was the mule, still tied to its post outside the dwelling. Had Temen or the boy been listening, they would've heard a neigh or a snuffle, hardly a greeting.

"Hey," the mule said again. "Are you dead?"

"NO."

"But he is?" the mule asked, presumably referring to Temen.

"YES."

"But not you."

The crow refused to answer the same question twice. That the mule would speak to it now was an indicator of its reduced status.

"I thought maybe you were dead because you rode on him and he rode on me. I wondered if maybe I was dead. But I would've remembered, I think.

What's it like, riding on a person? I dreamed it once. In my dream, I could stand on two legs. Do you dream?"

It hurt the crow to breathe. From inside the dwelling, the voices had dwindled to the occasional utterance. The light of the cookfire had begun to dim. The crow wondered how much longer it had to live.

"Can you hear me?" the mule said.

The mule snorted then, an involuntary sound. It also pranced as something small darted between its legs—a pika, making an indirect path to where the crow lay. At the sound of this disturbance, the human boy poked his head out. He surveyed the scene, put down some water for the mule, and retreated inside.

The pika sat on its haunches. It resumed their conversation from long ago. "My brother was our mother's favorite. This I could not change. But what if there was no brother, stone? Which of us would she love better, herself or me? Maybe her love for me would grow. If not, maybe it would look bigger without her love for him. So, I ate my brother. It made me sad...but not really. He was my brother because of our mother, not for any other reason. He kept her for himself too long. He—"

The pika froze. Then it was gone, zigzagging for the nearest shelter.

A moment later, the crow heard the sound of wings. At first, it thought of its ancestors in the netherworld, how they'd all plunged into the sea, but the crow wasn't dead yet. At least, it didn't think so. These wings were larger than a crow's.

Two vultures landed on the roof of the dwelling. They promptly folded their wings and craned their necks. The mule shuffled its feet, but this time, the boy didn't come to see. All was silent from inside the dwelling.

"What is it?" the first vulture asked. Its voice was terrible—a reckoning like no other sound in nature.

"A bird, I think," said the second vulture.

The crow tried to remain still.

"A bird? Impossible."

"Look at it. What else could it be?"

The first vulture took a step to its right, scattering grains from the roof. "If it's a bird, why doesn't it fly?"

"It is a bird," the mule volunteered. "It—"

The second vulture flapped its wings. "Silence, meat!" it cried, loud enough for the crow to tremble where it lay. "Maybe it's dead?"

The first vulture sniffed the air, rotating its head in a full circle. "I smell death," it said, "but inside. Rotten. Putrid. Not here. You, there, what's your name? Do you have a name?"

The question wasn't rhetorical. Convention

varied among species; some birds didn't believe in names, while others bequeathed more than one.

Among crows, it was tradition for a bird to choose its own name, at such a time that it truly knew itself, and then share its decision with the murder. If the murder felt it was appropriate, the name would become widely used. If it seemed vague or vainglorious, the murder would reject it, leaving the namebearer to make a decision—continue to know itself in this private way or accept the censure of its peers.

The crow hadn't arrived at a name until its fifth year. *WantsFor.* Even then, it had kept this designation to itself, until, finally, a new name had been assigned by the murder—*NoOne*. Though the intent had been to deride it, the crow hadn't minded. In fact, the two titles suited each other well, representative of a public and private self. In its own mind, the crow had become *WantsForNoOne*. It had never revealed itself to anyone. Not its murder, not the gods—not even the wind. Until now.

"CAW."

It didn't matter that the vultures spoke another language. It didn't matter if the mule was an idiot, or if the pika, still cowering in the bushes, was able to hear. The crow's name was a sound and that sound was unique to this bird. The crow emptied its lungs again—

"CAW"

—and with this declaration felt itself to be partially restored.

Everything hurt. The crow had been damaged beyond repair—by recent violence, yes, but also by the absence of its tailfeather. It couldn't be saved. Soon it would die, forever incomplete, forever in mourning, but it would travel to the netherworld as *WantsForNoOne,* a bird in possession of itself.

"What's it doing?" the first vulture said.

The crow had begun to drag itself toward the dwelling. Its destination seemed impossibly far away. However, should it arrive, it had one final deed in mind.

It required considerable effort to move its body. One of its wings was unresponsive. No matter how the crow entreated it, the appendage wouldn't extend. Mainly, the crow pushed with its legs. After the past few days in the natural world, it had gained a grudging respect for draft animals, and even humans, who spent so much of their time walking to and fro—not that the crow would've voiced those feelings aloud, even in the waning moments of its life.

The dwelling seemed closer now. In the foreground, the mule continued to shuffle its feet, while the vultures stared down from their perch. Would they eat the crow's corpse? it wondered. There was little meat left on its bones. But that was how an animal survived, by eating what was available, rather than waiting for some elusive bounty. Who understood this better than *WantsFor*, whose belly had never been entirely full?

Furthermore, a vulture would be loath to leave anything for a jackal to find. Better they become delirious with hunger that they might lead the carrion birds to unexpected fare, or else become a meal themselves.

"Bird," the second vulture hollered. "Where are you going?"

The crow could either respond or persevere. It didn't have the energy required for both.

Finally, it arrived at the threshold. Here, it paused for a moment to amass its strength. Inside, it could hear the tutting of the embers while the sleeping people breathed a steady rhythm. One sleeping person, to be precise. Temen no longer had need or reason to breathe, being a mitu, further evinced by his lack of snoring. The boy snored loudly enough for two. He laid on the floor, close to his new master. The mitu lay beside the cookfire—closer than the crow would've advised, given the dryness of Temen's skin. Too close and he might get singed.

There was no reason to delay. The crow dragged itself to the cookfire. When learning to fly, long ago, it had worried about venturing too near the sun before learning that such fears were unwarranted. Only in stories did a bird suffer the sun's embrace, and now, the crow solicited such a fate.

The cookfire was all but dormant. In order to reach its embers, the crow had to force aside a log that still glowed along its underbelly. The first time it touched an ember, it flinched. Here was real pain. Outside, it knew, the vultures would get a whiff. Would they guess what the crow had in mind? Would the mule? Who would free the beast from its post, and did the crow even care?

Once the embers had been exposed, the crow made itself a nest. The agony was exquisite. It brought to mind every hurt the crow had ever experienced prior to Temen—a hornet's sting, the collective effort of an ant colony, wounds from a kite hawk. The crow bathed in pain.

Its feathers made a noise like kindling. It could feel itself combust. Thankfully, for the time being, the crow was able to see. It wanted to enjoy the spectacle.

The point was not to die. That would happen, too, but first the crow had to make one last flight. While it still had life in its body, while it was still able to rise, *WantsForNoOne* pushed itself free of the cookfire.

Its feathers were no longer black, but a conflagration of color—red, yellow, and orange, but also green and blue. White. Purple. A spectrum. It wasn't a bird, moving on its own two feet. It was a vengeful ghost, terrible and playful, come to visit this dwelling and burn it to the ground.

The crow hop-flapped as it had in the orchard. Now, it could no longer see. But as it flailed in the confined space, throwing its body against the walls and the wicker storage containers—even brushing the ceiling in one inspired leap—it could hear the vultures sound the alarm, flapping their enormous wings as they departed from their roost, and the despondent mule, tethered to his doom. Cries from the boy, who woke to searing heat. It didn't hear Temen, who couldn't smell or feel, but located the mitu nevertheless. He was lying on the floor, untroubled by the commotion.

The burning crow rubbed itself against Temen's dress. It caressed the mitu's parchment-like skin. Because he didn't have hair, the crow sought out his eyebrows, eager to disfigure his face.

Whether as a result of being jostled, or because the blaze was now roaring, Temen finally stirred. All at once, he hurled the crow away, having been perched on the mitu's chest. Temen wailed.

The crow, blinded, imagined him stumbling toward the door, if the door was even visible. It imagined Temen walking into the night—a sight to behold, this blazing person. Even if he found his way to an irrigation canal, it would be too late. Temen was bound for the netherworld, this time to stay.

The crow collapsed. *WantsForNoOne,* also bound for that place. How would it be seen? Charred—like a piece of dung burned for warmth. The bird was amused by this.

Not a bird. Anymore.

22

MESHARA

IT WAS EXACTLY what she'd feared; Ziz had been imprisoned, Hazi wanted blood, and there was nothing Meshara could do.

If anything was working in their favor, it was the surprising autonomy of the High Zagmi. As the final arbiter of Ziz's innocence or guilt, he'd refused to cede to Hazi's will but had instead confined Ziz to her quarters and conducted his own series of interviews. He'd even assigned her to the temple of Ninhursag, where she'd be guarded by stewards to the goddess—a safer place, no doubt, than Hazi's compound.

"This is absurd." Hazi berated the High Zagmi as if he were a child. Remembering her place, she modulated her tone. "She's a murderer. She doesn't deserve mercy."

The High Zagmi looked uncomfortable in his red linen, or he was hungry. Hazi had provided finger foods, same as before, but these were less grand, perhaps because she no longer had Meshara to shop with.

Along with her daughter, Meshara had been expelled from the compound. She, too, was a guest of the temple, summoned today for reasons that hadn't been explained to her yet.

She quietly made a survey of her surroundings. There was less variety among the fruits. Even the quality of slaves serving the food had deteriorated. Gone were the buxom young women from before, the ones that had so pleased the High Zagmi, now replaced by an adolescent boy. The priest eyed both the child and the food with suspicion.

Meshara hadn't thought of the High Zagmi as someone who would stand on principle. Even now, she failed to see his motivation—perhaps the disdain he'd shown for Garash in the past? If the man didn't answer to Hazi, then he must answer to the gods. If this was true, and he was mindful of his responsibility, then maybe she and Ziz had a chance after all.

The High Zagmi cleared his throat. He made no move toward the food. "What we know," he said, "is very little. We do not know if Garash is dead. Your son claims to have seen him in the netherworld, but he can't prove that. The girl, so far, has refused to speak. We can confirm that these people worked on Garash's land, and that he traveled there for purposes we do not know—"

"To arrange a marriage to her," Hazi said. "Which she, the serpent—"

"We do not know," the High Zagmi emphasized. "The only person who could answer any of these questions isn't here. However, I have sent soldiers to the farm. What they will find will inform my decision. Once we know if your husband is dead or alive—"

Again, Hazi interrupted the holy man. "You listen very carefully," she said with a sneer. "That man was my husband. Now he's gone. I know this because I feel it—he is missing from this world. That snake killed him. I don't know how she did it, but she did. She's lied and taken advantage of me ever since. Her and *her*."

With this, she indicted Meshara, the silent party in the room. Meshara blanched. The invitation, which had actually been a summons, had come from the High Zagmi. Meshara wasn't present at Hazi's request, nor did she expect to be treated well. She'd hoped to remain as circumspect as possible.

"Yes," the High Zagmi also acknowledged her. "The girl's mother—the only person, not counting the girl, who was present when Garash visited the farm. If, indeed, he visited the farm. The only other person who may possess answers."

The High Zagmi had spoken to Meshara once since Ziz was taken—about the details of the arranged marriage, questions that Meshara had been unable to answer. Temen hadn't told her. She didn't know.

Now, she swallowed. She wondered whether she was allowed to eat the food, regardless of its quality. The temple only served lentils, which always reminded her of their treatment upon arrival. She could barely choke down a mouthful.

"Did you witness Garash's death?"

These words were spoken by the High Zagmi. Hazi stared at Meshara with withering intensity.

"No," she said.

"Did you see his body? Do you know for a fact that he's dead?"

"No," she said again. "I don't know any of these things."

"She's lying," Hazi insisted.

The High Zagmi gave Meshara a skeptical look.

"Anyone who would lie in the presence of the gods doesn't fear mortal punishment. They will endure far worse in the next life."

It was a statement to test her conviction, but what other truth did she possess? Ziz had run back to the dwelling, distraught. She'd claimed Garash was dead by some kind of animal attack—a leopard?

Meshara had believed her. She *still* believed her, though she hadn't seen the body. To confess what little she knew would only support the accusations made against her daughter while further undermining her own security, without the added benefit of clarity. Meshara looked for something to eat, but the boy bearing the platter had gone.

"I never saw him," she said.

"Liar!" Hazi shouted, but apparently the High Zagmi had heard enough.

"The soldiers will go to the farm," he said. "After they've learned what there is to learn, they will return. Justice will be served according to fact, and not—"

Hazi opened her mouth to speak, but the High Zagmi raised his own voice, the furrows in his scalp deepening—

"—not on the basis of theory. In the meantime, the girl will stay at the temple. Pray for a speedy resolution."

Having said all he intended to say, the holy man turned to leave. Meshara understood his hasty retreat. He seemed unlikely to benefit from Hazi's hospitality, but she wished he would've taken her with him. The man had given no thought to Meshara's predicament, though it was he who'd summoned her in the first place—typical behavior for someone in power, especially a man. Her frustration at the outcome was so familiar that Meshara barely noticed it.

In his absence, only the women remained. At first, Hazi didn't acknowledge Meshara. She appeared too consumed by her own feelings. Meshara considered following the High Zagmi out. More than considered it—her legs almost carried her in that direction.

But what better opportunity to beg for mercy? Beg she would—Ziz had imperiled them both and Hazi would be the chief advocate for any punishment.

"Hazi," Meshara began.

"Do not."

Yet she persisted. "Our children are meant to be married," she said. "We're already family—we're sisters, you and I. We know what a family can endure. It's only by remaining loyal to each other that the worst circumstances can be overcome. Look at me. When I first came here—"

"I gave you everything. Clothes to wear. Your freedom."

Meshara bristled at the word. What freedom did she really possess, living at the beck and call of another person? A place to stay—this she had requested. But mourning clothes? Her freedom from Temen?

Her husband was dead, of this Meshara was certain, whether or not the world cared to accept it. What greater freedom had she gained, especially now? If anything, she'd sacrificed a piece of herself. The tip of her finger—inconsequential to someone else, but not its owner. Not when she remained trapped. How could this be considered freedom?

"You were very generous," she agreed, though she spoke through clenched teeth. "In that spirit, I ask you—"

"No."

Hazi turned and strode out of the room. Without thinking, Meshara followed after her.

"Is it possible," she asked the rich woman's back, "that you're better off without Garash?"

Hazi abruptly stopped. She turned to face Meshara. The two of them crowded the hallway, should anyone have been so brave as to pass.

"Whether or not he's dead," Meshara continued, "look what you've accomplished. Look how well you're received. You don't need Garash for that."

Hazi laughed. "What do you know of power?" she said. "You've never had it, not for a second. Do you know how people would treat me if Garash wasn't my husband? Or if I became his widow? I was the daughter of a fruit-seller. I *am* the daughter of a fruit-seller—I always will be, no matter what. People don't forget. You think the High Zagmi has? You see how he treats me in my own home. No, they wait. They wait until you're weak, and then they take everything away."

A wide range of emotions played across Hazi's face. Meshara could empathize with them all—anger, resentment, humiliation. She'd experienced the full gamut during her altercation in the kitchen. The emotion that troubled her most, that inspired a person to make the worst decisions, was fear.

Hazi resumed her stride—toward the kitchen, apparently. Meshara kept pace, speaking to her back when the other woman refused to acknowledge her.

"Then show them strength. Your mercy will be a demonstration of power."

"No. There will be no mercy."

"You'd kill her? She's only a child, Hazi—she's done nothing wrong."

Her matron stopped again. They were standing in one of the compound's many open-ceilinged courtyards, this one serving no other purpose than to join a confluence of passageways. Overhead, the sky was grey. Elsewhere in Nippur, people would be arranging pots and urns outside at the rare chance of rain, hoping to catch the sweet run-off for bathing water and soup stock. Children like Ziz would be raising their faces with open mouths.

"Kill her?" Hazi said. "I will make her my slave. She'll right her wrongs through a lifetime of service. Not in the kitchen. Not in the shadows. Anywhere I go, she will follow. Everyone will see that the child who killed Garash was made to surrender own life. Even after I remarry. Even after my death. I will take any future she might've had, no matter how paltry."

"But Wasu—"

"Wasu can have her if he wants. You think he doesn't pick and choose from the slaves already? That he hasn't since he was a child? How else would he learn?"

Meshara was horrified. For a moment, she thought the rain had begun, but it was only the sensation of being dappled, her flesh buzzing in a hundred different places. She couldn't imagine the future Hazi had described.

"You are a mother," she heard herself say. "Please. My child—"

"Don't compare us," Hazi hissed. "We are nothing alike. My advice to you is go—take advantage of your freedom. Find another man. Have more children."

"But Ziz—"

"Forget her."

Hazi took a step closer.

"Take yourself from this place. Go to Uruk or Kish. Someplace new. Because when the soldiers return, if they say you were involved in my husband's death, I will kill you too. In a public place, where everyone can see. I will do it myself—with my own teeth."

Hazi leaned forward. Meshara wondered what she meant to do—whether she'd enact the threat—but instead, the rich woman nuzzled her, even wrapped her arms around Meshara's waist and squeezed. It seemed they stood this way for an eternity.

THERE WOULD BE NO REPRIEVE. Hazi's heart couldn't be softened, and the High Zagmi, despite his devotion to justice, wasn't likely to be lenient. Ziz would suffer the life of a slave, while Meshara's own fate might be even more brutal.

At least she was allowed to visit Ziz. The stewards had been inhospitable during their previous encounters, but Meshara didn't mind. Hospitality, now, seemed like a foreign concept to her. Keeping her eyes down and speaking to no one, she entered the temple.

She carried her possessions in a burlap scrap—items that Ziz had requested. Meshara couldn't recall gathering them from Hazi's compound. Her mind was unable to focus, still reeling from her matron's touch. She had only days, at best, until the soldiers returned. If she didn't decide on a course of action, it would soon be too late.

Meshara proceeded down a stairwell. She continued past the level that housed the dining hall, deeper into the ziggurat. Ziz was being held in a storage room. There were no actual jail cells in the temple. The zagmi didn't make a habit of detaining people. Soldiers were responsible for meting out justice, often swiftly and brutally. They acted on behalf of whoever wielded power, an arrangement that made perverse sense.

Meshara thought about what Hazi had said, about killing her herself, and had to suppress a shiver. Perhaps it would be better to die by a soldier's hand, a person who felt no animosity toward her? It was gruesome to even consider such a question.

A young steward was posted outside Ziz's door. There was always someone, a person whose job was less to detain Ziz than to observe her visitors.

Meshara could've subdued this particular woman herself. She was waif-thin, with close-set eyes and a stained, black tongue. Previously, Meshara had encountered an elderly woman by the door. She noted the discrepancy.

"I'm here for my daughter," she said. She was unsure whether she had to identify herself.

The steward scowled at her. "What's that?" she said, eying the parcel.

Meshara obediently turned back the corners, thinking, as she did so, that this represented a second deviation. "A feather and some berries?"

The steward glanced down to confirm, then stepped aside.

The storage room was guarded by a heavy wooden door. This was its only qualification as a jail cell, this and the absence of windows, so far below the surface. The air inside was stagnant from poor ventilation. Shelves lined the walls, while palettes on the floor made uneven shadows.

"Ziz?" Meshara whispered.

The steward promptly closed the door behind her.

When her daughter moved into the light, Meshara thought she looked unwell. Her eyes were sunken and her cheeks were gaunt. She couldn't have lost weight in such a short period of time, could she? What were they feeding her?

"Step forward," Meshara said, opening her arms. "Let me see you."

Ziz embraced her without ardor. She felt less substantial.

In her head, Meshara enumerated a dozen apologies to her daughter—that she, Meshara, had allowed Temen to dictate their futures, that they'd both suffered as a result of his temper and greed. These apologies went unmade.

Stepping free of their embrace, she held her daughter at arm's length. "Hazi won't be reasonable," Meshara said. "She wants justice."

Briefly, she considered the possibility that they were being spied upon—that she should choose her words more carefully—but the room hadn't been designed with subterfuge in mind. Either way, troves of centuries-old lagan absorbed any noise that she and Ziz might create.

"Justice?" Ziz echoed, as if the word carried no meaning. "What does that mean?"

Meshara licked her lips. Grudgingly, she confessed, "The High Zagmi has sent soldiers to investigate Garash's death. He won't allow anything to happen until they've returned. But if they think you had anything to do with it—"

"What? What happens then?"

Meshara shook her head, as if to dispel the notion. "Hazi is being unreasonable," she repeated, "and there's no way to escape."

Ziz nodded. The scant light of the room made it difficult to see her eyes. "Did you bring the things I asked for?"

Meshara handed over the parcel, wondering again if they were being spied upon before reminding herself that the steward had already examined the package.

"Why the berries?" she asked. If Ziz had previously mentioned their purpose, Meshara had forgotten.

"To stain my tongue," her daughter replied. She folded back the burlap to make an inventory of its contents. "Wasu and I did it once, together."

"You think it may soften his feelings?"

"Maybe."

"Aren't there other uses for them? The stewards at the temple—they do more than just stain their tongues."

Ziz glanced at her mother and quickly looked away. So she did know—too many berries, when consumed at once, could be poisonous.

Meshara wondered what use her daughter had planned for them. Did she intend to make Wasu sick? Or else to murder him? More importantly, did she, Meshara, desire an answer to these questions, or was she best served by remaining ignorant?

"And the tailfeather?" she said.

Ziz held up the feather in question, white and belonging to a crow, if one believed that such things could be obtained. Meshara thought it looked more like a gull's feather.

"Did you have trouble getting it?" Ziz asked.

Meshara frowned at the question. "No," she said.

"It was in a pile with some other things. It didn't seem to have any special significance. What's it for?"

"It was a gift," Ziz replied, as if this would satisfy Meshara's curiosity. Carefully, she folded down the corners of the parcel and carried it across the room, where she'd arranged a sleeping mat for herself on the floor.

"There's no way to flee this place," Meshara asserted, changing the subject. Perhaps, if her daughter understood, she would suggest the obvious course of action—that Meshara make an effort to save herself. "No secret passageways," she continued, "a guard at every door—"

"Is Temen dead?"

The question stopped her cold. Meshara stroked her missing digit with its corresponding thumb.

"Yes."

Ziz looked at her. It was impossible to read her face. "Are you sure?" she said.

Meshara didn't hesitate a second time. "Yes—he left us. He's not coming back."

"So, he's in the netherworld?"

"Yes, Ziz," she agreed with a sigh, "but not us. We're stuck. I've pleaded with the High Zagmi, but Hazi is determined. Even if the soldiers don't find proof, she'll continue searching until she locates Garash's attendant, and who knows what he'll say? If she brings him here, she can put thoughts in his head—or maybe she'll kill him, too. Sooner or later, she's bound to get what she wants. You understand all this, yes? It's you that she wants. "

Ziz smiled. Meshara weakly returned the gesture, wondering if it entailed a permission of sorts.

"Tell me the story of An and Ninhursag?"

"What? Why?"

Ziz made herself a seat on the floor. "I'd just like to hear it."

Meshara sighed. It was unclear whether her daughter didn't understand or didn't *want* to understand. So much had gone unsaid between them—to tease out one thread risked unraveling the entire tapestry. Perhaps a story was for the best, one in which the outcome was predetermined.

"Very well," Meshara said. "Move aside."

Taking a seat next to Ziz, she began to narrate.

"In the time before time, the goddess Ninhursag lived on the banks of the Euphrates. There, she chased frogs and ate honey cakes all day and spent her time blissfully alone. But the god An watched from afar. He bore witness to her solitude and imagined it was something he could possess, like a blanket or a spade. He decided to marry her and make her contentment his own."

Meshara looked at Ziz's face—her daughter seemed rapt. It had been a long time since she'd told this story. She wondered how much Ziz had retained.

"Do you remember what Ninhursag said?"

"She said no."

"That's right," Meshara agreed. "She said no. 'Why get married?' she said. 'I have everything I need.' But this wasn't the answer that An wanted. He waited until she was sleeping, then dragged her by the hair to the highest peak of Mashu, where he lived in a palace."

Meshara continued, "When Ninhursag woke up and saw where she was, she immediately knew what had happened. An wasn't the first to woo her—nor, she suspected, would he be the last. So, before he woke, she decided to teach him a lesson. She would change her appearance."

"But," Ziz protested, anticipating this twist. "Couldn't she have become a bird? Or a poisonous snake, to bite him on the toe?"

"Yes, she could've become those things," Meshara agreed, running her hand through her daughter's hair. "She could've attacked him or fled, but the goddess was wise. She knew that protesting would only make matters worse. The decision to spare her had to originate with An."

"But—"

"Would you like me to tell the story?"

For a moment, Ziz sulked, but then she nodded her head.

Meshara also nodded. It was important that Ziz understood Ninhursag did what was necessary to ensure her freedom. She was clever and resourceful, an example to women everywhere. "Good," Meshara said. "The goddess pulled out her hair and all of her teeth. Then she roused An. When the god saw what she'd become, he reacted with horror. 'Who are you?' he shouted. 'It's me, your wife.' 'You aren't my wife—you're ugly!' And he forced Ninhursag to leave his palace and return to the banks of the Euphrates."

There was a knock at the storeroom door. Both women started. Meshara's visit was nearing its end.

"Do you remember what happens next?" she asked.

Ziz shrugged her shoulders. "She stays that way."

"Except when she looks in the Euphrates. Only then can see her reflection as it truly was."

Meshara delivered this conclusion with all the enthusiasm she could muster, and still it fell flat.

"Don't you see?" she said, feeling a spasm of contempt for her ignorant child. "Ninhursag is the hero of the story!"

Ziz regarded her stoically. Choosing her words with evident care, she said, "Yes, I see, but I don't understand. Why doesn't she just die?"

23

ZIZ

HER MOTHER DEPARTED SOON THEREAFTER. Ziz was neither happy nor sad to see her go. She knew it was probably the last time they'd meet in the natural world, but she couldn't share that information with Meshara, lest she stymy her plans—a likely scenario, given her mother's talk of escape.

Without a final farewell, Ziz was left feeling incomplete. Everything seemed to have a greater significance, she thought, now that she was close to death. But really, life was the same from one moment to the next, until it ceased to be. It was only a matter of perspective.

Meshara had brought what she'd asked for. For this, Ziz was grateful. There were more than enough berries to poison herself.

Ziz picked up the tailfeather and held it before

her eyes. She was pained it had been so easy to acquire. She'd expected Wasu to guard it more closely, but perhaps that had been its only appeal—Ziz's reluctance to part with it. Minus that, it was just another trinket for someone in possession of more than his share.

Holding the quill between her thumb and finger, Ziz twirled it, delighting in the sound it made. If Wasu didn't see the value of this totem, she certainly did.

On the second day of her confinement, she'd realized she'd never be free again.

Ziz was accused of murder. Her dialogue with the High Zagmi had made it clear that he presumed her guilt—and, in truth, wasn't she guilty of something? Yes, she'd led Garash to the ravine—she'd watched him die. Whether she was subsequently put to death or made a slave, she'd receive some form of punishment for her role in these events, and that punishment would result in the loss of freedom.

But how free had she been to begin with? What constituted freedom? Ziz had thought back as far as she could, and she found it difficult to remember a time when she'd belonged to herself. Always there was Temen, the father who would determine her future.

Thus, she'd made a plan. She would eat the berries they'd used to stain their tongues—she'd convinced Meshara to provide them, under the pretense of making amends with Wasu. When she reached the netherworld, she'd locate her father. Temen would grant her her freedom. Then, using the tailfeather, Ziz would find her way back.

She knew this last part would be difficult—she didn't know how the magic worked. But even if she became stranded in the netherworld, she sullenly mused, how would that be worse than her current predicament?

The stewards almost never checked on her. Still, Ziz took precautions. She sat with her weight against the storeroom door. It wouldn't prevent two or more adults from entering, but it would gain her some time. She didn't know how long the berries took to work.

Like before, with Wasu, she shoved as many in her mouth as possible.

Ziz chewed to release the berries' juices and waited for her tongue to grow numb. The taste was bitter. This time, she intentionally swallowed a mouthful, keeping the greater portion in her cheeks. She wondered if she'd have to eat all the berries to—

Something happened. Her legs shot out, locking at the knees. Ziz tried to massage them, to coax the muscles into a more relaxed state, but her arms also spasmed. They were bouncing—shoulders lifting, hands flailing. Her jaw locked. She inadvertently slammed her head against the door, once, twice. Again. Again. She could hear the steward saying something on the outside, but she couldn't make out the words. Ziz's cheeks were burning. Her stomach was in knots.

Pitching forward, she collapsed on the floor. As her vision blurred, she thought, Of course, because I swallowed—

Ziz seized so hard that her spine bowed. Thankfully, she'd lost consciousness before her bowels emptied and her tongue blocked off the flow of oxygen to her lungs. In less than two minutes, Ziz was dead.

It was as if the memory of the storeroom were replaced by this charred landscape.

A layer of ash covered her ankles. Sparse trees stood nearby, gnarled under the pressure of intense heat. Whatever conflagration had caused this scene had already passed, but the sky above was hazy and red.

Even before she opened her mouth, Ziz could taste the acrid smell of smoke on her tongue—which, she could see, had been stained in the process of poisoning herself.

Poisoning herself. Ziz was dead.

Frantically, she searched for the tailfeather, only to find it clutched in her right hand. Its hue matched that of the ashes. Were she to drop it, she might not find it again.

Holding it to her chest, Ziz surveyed her surroundings. If this was the netherworld, where were all the people? Had they all been burned up in the fire or had they fled? How was she supposed to find Temen? She'd anticipated the problem of returning to the natural world, but she hadn't considered this dilemma, locating her father among the other mitu. At the very least, she'd expected there to *be* other mitu.

"Hello?"

"Permission for everything," croaked a nearby tree.

Ziz jumped. The tree had eyes. It had a mouth.

The tree said, "Permission to leave. Permission to stay. Permission to use a bucket—for bathing, for anything. It didn't matter. Permission to ask permission was the joke. But not really. Once a thing was permissible, it went back to being impermissible, until permission was granted again. Or not. Always the possibility of not."

The tree wasn't a tree at all, Ziz saw, but a mitu—taller than a person in real life and deprived of hair and clothes, which, presumably, had been consumed in the blaze. The mitu watched her as she retreated a step—into a second mitu, equally tall, though broader and stooped over.

This one said, "All I ask is that you listen. Will you listen? How will I know? I'll know if you can repeat what I said—not the words but their meaning. Anyone can repeat the words. To listen, one must hear. To hear, one must—"

"Temen?" Ziz called.

"Ziz?"

Her father's voice emerged from the other side of this mitu-tree. Ziz walked around it, where she discovered a second pair of features angled upward toward the glowing sky. It didn't look like Temen.

For a moment, she wondered if her mind was playing tricks on her. Did she even have a mind? How much of herself had she retained after she'd died?

"Ziz?" the mitu-tree said again. This time, she was sure it was Temen's voice. He couldn't see her, given the direction he was facing, but he craned his eyes. "Is that you?"

"Father?"

"What're you doing here?"

His question was delivered in such a tone of a rebuke that Ziz cringed. She decided not to tell him about the berries, or anything else about the natural world, for that matter. She was here because she was dead, that much should've been obvious. She was dead, by her own hand, with an express purpose.

"Father?" she said again. "I don't belong to you. I belong to me—only me."

Ziz wished he could see her better. She wondered if he'd heard her—and, if he had, what his response might be. Although she'd carefully rehearsed this statement, her voice had trembled as she spoke the words aloud.

Sure enough, Temen replied, "What? What are you saying? What are you doing here? Ziz, did something happen to you?"

"I belong to me," she said again, gaining confidence. "Not to you or anyone else."

Did she require his consent? If she truly believed what she was saying, then she wasn't Temen's to surrender. It didn't matter if he agreed or not, or if he even grasped the meaning of her words.

Which begged the question—why make the trip? Why go to the pain of killing herself if an audience with Temen hadn't been necessary?

Because she wanted him to know. Because she wanted to speak the words, to feel them articulated in her posture, and to depart this place knowing she'd represented her freedom.

"You shouldn't be here," he said. "You need to go home. You, bird—take her away."

Temen shook one of his tree limbs, which, Ziz thought, might constitute an arm. At the end dangled a strange protrusion, almost like a scorched fruit. But, similar to the mitu themselves, this object was bigger than any fruit she'd ever seen. Temen's tree limb trembled until the fruit came loose. It landed with a thud, raising a cloud of white ash. Ziz coughed.

"You," Temen scolded the lump. "This is my daughter. Take her back to the natural world—she doesn't belong here."

Ziz leaned over to examine the thing. It didn't resemble a fruit so much as a blackened wasp nest.

"MINE."

Ziz stood upright. "It talked!" she exclaimed.

"MINE."

"What have you got?" Temen asked her.

His question didn't register at first—Ziz was too busy gaping at the object. Was anything in this place what it appeared to be? Talking trees, talking lumps—

"What are you holding?"

"Nothing," she said. "A feather."

"Give it to the crow."

"A crow?"

To the extent that an inanimate object could appear agitated, this object did. It was rocking to and fro, like it was trying to propel itself forward. Ziz looked at the feather in her hand. The feather didn't behave in an outlandish manner. The feather, which she'd bargained would gain her readmittance to the natural world, seemed to be only and exactly a feather.

"Give it."

Not knowing what else to do, Ziz extended the tailfeather toward the crow—or what her father, who was a mitu who was also a tree, insisted on calling a crow. The crow lacked hands or any visible aperture, so Ziz resolved to puncture its surface.

In the final moment, she hesitated, her hand poised. What if Temen was wrong? What if she lost the tailfeather as a result and, with it, her ability to go home? These concerns were valid but unknowable.

Thus, with every intention of leaving this place, and not simply because her father had said so, Ziz inserted the quill.

Immediately, the crow changed—it became a crow. Its black, irregular surface was replaced by white feathers. The bird spread its wings and cawed. It even pecked at Ziz's outstretched hand, which she hastily withdrew. The crow angled its neck in a way that appeared uncomfortable to appraise its body—perhaps searching for the tailfeather that Ziz had provided. Then it flapped its wings and hopped, leaving the ground and coming to rest a few feet away.

"CAW. CAW."

"Yes, yes, good for you," Temen snapped. "Now get her away."

The crow flapped its wings again and ascended. Ziz watched it rise. The crow, she thought, was beautiful. It had also stolen the tailfeather she'd intended to bring her back. Admiration and disappointment spoke in each ear, leaving her with conflicted feelings. Would she become a tree like Temen now? Was there more to the netherworld than this?

When the bird had traveled far enough that it resembled only a white dot, it turned and flew back toward her. Ziz knew this because she observed it getting larger. Down it came, pressing its wings to its sides and falling like a spear. Panic proved to be Ziz's loudest emotion, drowning out her other feelings. She wondered how the bird would arrest itself, until she realized, at the very last moment, that it wouldn't.

The crow punctured her sternum, the force of its impact turning her inside-out. Like the experience in the storeroom, the memory of this place was substituted for darkness. On all sides, she was surrounded by space, like a tiny vessel on a great sea. She didn't know how she knew this without the benefit of sight, only that her knowledge was secure.

"Where are we?" she asked.

"THE SPACE BETWEEN."

She recognized the crow's voice—and while she was surprised and even alarmed that it could speak, she was nonetheless grateful for the bird's company.

"In between where?"

"THE NETHERWORLD AND THE NATURAL WORLD, WHERE YOU WILL REMAIN. I HEARD HIM CALL YOU DAUGHTER. THE CHILD OF A MONSTER HAS THE MONSTER WITHIN. IT IS NOT YOUR FAULT—IT CANNOT BE HELPED. BUT I WON'T TAKE YOU ANY FARTHER."

Ziz bristled. She wished she could see her accuser so she could at least scowl at it. "If you heard all that," she argued, "then you heard me say I don't belong to him."

"I HEARD."

To Ziz's ear, it sounded like an admission. "Then don't punish me for being his daughter. If you want to leave me, fine, but not because of him. I'll find my own way, alone."

"Not alone," a third voice corrected her.

Ziz experienced a bodily sensation, though she was lacking a body, or perhaps it was her body's way of asserting itself. Her heart beat faster. Again, panic made itself known.

She recognized the voice. It had come from where she would've had ears, had she ears. The voice belonged to Garash.

"Why do you hide, child?" he chided her. "Didn't

the bird explain? You can be anything you want here. Look at me."

Then Ziz could see him—Garash, but younger than the man she'd known, leaner and with fewer lines in his face. He was dressed as a soldier, with dried blood smeared across his cheeks and the familiar stone cylinder clenched in his palm. The sight of this object, more than anything else, inspired in her feelings of shame and disgust.

Garash was a locus. Suddenly, she wasn't lost in space—Ziz existed at a relative distance from this threat, and that distance wasn't great enough. Her body was a weakness that could be exploited. She was a hindrance to herself.

Before she could determine the mechanics of self-propulsion, Garash had accosted her, giving Ziz form with his uninvited touch.

"I recognize you, daughter," he said. "Have you seen my son?"

She now possessed a wrist where he'd seized her. She had a shoulder where she struggled to free herself and teeth that gnashed in alarm.

Garash pulled her closer. The sensation was like floating on water. Ziz helplessly drifted until she was close enough for him to choke. Garash was pressing the stone cylinder against her neck in an effort to strangle her.

"Did he send you here? Did he kill you for what

you did to me? Did you think it would end? A person can die many times, I've learned. You will see."

"YOUR NECK."

Fearful, flailing, Ziz strained to see the crow. With Garash's hands upon her, it was impossible to turn her head, but her eyes darted to and fro. Her lungs burned for air. Her tongue, presumably still black, felt listless in her mouth.

"YOUR NECK," the crow repeated. Then she saw it—a streak of white in the ether. "YOU DON'T HAVE ONE."

What? she thought, or tried to think, the voice in her head becoming frayed and shrill.

"YOU DON'T HAVE A NECK. HE CANNOT STRANGLE YOU WITHOUT A NECK. IN THIS PLACE, YOU DECIDE."

"Shut up, bird," Garash snarled. "I decide. The girl will receive her punishment, and you—"

In another streak, the crow darted past Ziz and through Garash, leaving a hole in the soldier's abdomen. He reacted as if he'd been struck, his body folding around the wound. Ziz thought it might force his hands from her throat, but then she reflected on what the bird had said. When had she regained corporeal form? When Garash had touched her, had he brought her into being, or had she?

"You stabbed me!" Garash thundered, even as the

crow made a second pass, piercing the soldier's shoulder.

Ziz ignored her lungs. All at once, she could breathe again—or, more to the point, she wasn't struggling to breathe. Similarly, she ignored her wrists, sore from where they'd been cuffed. She ignored her eyes and her tongue. When she ignored her throat, her final sensation was of Garash's hands passing through her. The soldier gaped at the place where she'd just been.

"Come back!" he howled. "Where did you go?"

"I THINK HE DID NOT HEAR YOU," the crow remarked, "WHEN YOU SAID YOU BELONGED TO YOURSELF. I THINK HE BELIEVES IT TO BE UNTRUE."

The bird shot through the soldier's torso again and again, like threading a piece of leather. With each pass, Garash lost a chunk of himself, these holes refusing to close.

Now Ziz understood. It was Garash's insistence on form that empowered the crow. Because Garash was unwilling to abandon the idea of himself, he was vulnerable.

"ONE MOMENT," the crow said.

Again, it flew at Garash, this time through a preexisting hole. Ziz understood what she was seeing without being able to rationalize it—the rest of

Garash, what remained of him, was tugged along, so he too passed through the wound, cylinder and all, until both the crow and Garash had disappeared. There was even, to Ziz's satisfaction, a faint popping sound.

Then she was left alone. In the space between.

Without substance or form.

In however much time elapsed, Ziz began to think about herself, specifically the parts of herself that were missing. The arm where she'd been grabbed in the bazaar. The knees where Wasu had kissed her.

She didn't want her body back. It wasn't her body's fault; it had been resilient, but too much pain had been inflicted upon it, and the threat of more remained.

She thought of Meshara's finger, the one she'd cut off. Was this so very different? Instead of amputating one piece at a time, Ziz had sacrificed everything. She, too, had earned her freedom.

The crow returned with an identical pop.

"I BROUGHT HIM BACK TO THE NETHERWORLD. HE'LL BE CONFUSED BY HIS HOLES, BUT HE'LL TELL HIMSELF A NEW STORY. THEY ALL DO—THE STORY OF INEVITABILITY."

The crow floated in space. It seemed to know where to address itself—where to orient its head in order to speak to her. Did that mean Ziz existed in space, too, relative to the bird? Was she simply invisible?

"HOW DO I LOOK?"

Ziz considered the question.

Pretty.

"I THINK SO TOO." The crow held its wings apart from its body in order to examine them. "I'VE NEVER BEEN THIS COLOR BEFORE."

The tailfeather was white.

"IT WAS YOURS TO KEEP."

I didn't know how to use it.

"I'LL SHOW YOU."

Ziz was afraid. Surely, she'd suffered enough—was the bird proposing that she leave this place? Would she have to return to the storeroom? To Hazi's punishment or her arranged marriage to Wasu? Why not stay in the space between?

"THIS IS NO PLACE TO STAY," the crow insisted, as if it were privy to her private thoughts. Perhaps it could hear her think—Ziz didn't understand the rules.

Why not?

"THERE'S NOTHING LEFT TO HIDE FROM."

I don't want to be myself.

"THEN IMAGINE SOMETHING DIFFERENT. A DIFFERENT SHAPE."

Ziz conjured literal shapes—circles, squares, and

triangles. She might enjoy being a rectangle, she mused.

"DON'T BE STUPID," the crow scolded her. "THE WORLD IS HARSH—YOU MUST BE HARSHER. IMAGINE SOMETHING TO BE RECKONED WITH."

You'll show me?

"YOU SHOW ME. IMAGINE YOURSELF."

And so she did.

Ziz imagined herself as she'd appeared in Hazi's mirror, in a shapeless dress, with skinny limbs and a frizz of brown hair. She despised this person. She felt powerless and small.

She tried to imagine herself as larger, somehow—so large that her arms and legs were as long as people and twice as thick. But that idea was preposterous. How could she fit inside a home? Or walk down the street?

She returned to her initial form—the fragile girl defeated by the sight of her own reflection, or, rather, how she knew herself to be seen by others.

"NO," the crow encouraged her. "NOT AS YOU WERE—AS YOU WILL BE."

What was fierce? An animal was fierce. Could that be her new form? Ziz thought of the leopard that had murdered Garash. She thought of the crow pecking at her hand in the netherworld. She remembered the snakeskins from the bazaar. Then she recalled her dream, when Wasu had eaten her doll—the two of them huddled together in her parents' dwelling. The terror she'd experienced as something had stalked across her roof.

An Asag.

"YES."

As Ziz imagined it, she noticed something. Gently, slowly, the darkness was receding. Soon she'd be able to distinguish the outline of her body, but, for now, she was indistinct. What she saw were the burgeoning hues—pink and orange, warming the darkness.

Ziz imagined the Asag.

Her legs were a bird's talons. She observed how easily they tucked underneath her, whether in flight or repose, and the strength of their grip. Intuitively, she knew the sharpness of her claws. She could peel flesh like parting a curtain. She could injure, maim, or kill.

Exploring the rest of her body, she discovered reptilian skin. It covered the whole of her torso. Ziz was impervious—no water could seep in. No blade or shaft would ever cause her harm. The sun warmed her scales and reflected the light like a prism, a wondrous sight to behold.

She also had wings—white, like the crow's. They responded to her whim, yet somehow understood flight in a way that Ziz could not. Drag and loft.

Currents and thermals. She beat them, gaining altitude as she did, then coasted on the surprising buoyancy of the air. Every feather created its own wake, like fingers trailing through a stream.

"YES."

The crow had formed the natural world around them. For a while, it flew beside her, tiny by comparison, before it veered off in another direction.

Ziz continued on her own path, not knowing where she was going. To Nippur? To the dwelling? Far below, she could see the Euphrates River coursing toward the horizon, where great Mashu was nuzzled by clouds. It occurred to her that if she looked down, she'd see her own reflection in the water.

Like the goddess Ninhursag, if Ziz saw her true self, who would that be? The idea was exhilarating but also terrifying.

Ziz decided to be brave.

She looked down.

She was beautiful.

ACKNOWLEDGMENTS

Amr Abouelleil, Adam Benjamin, Crystal Calanca, Audra Carmine, Veda Carmine-Ritchie, Ellie Duclos-Yourdon, Teddy Duclos-Yourdon, Kate Fox, Samantha Gamboa, Liz Greenhill, Michael Keefe, Cody Luff, Yelena Malcolm, Elizabeth Marshea, Lara Messersmith-Glavin, Alex Minkow, Anatoly Molotkov, Toni Nash, Margaret Pinard, Dara Resnik, Sharon Rose, Laura Stanfill, Tammy Lynne Stoner, Jon Wasserman, and Rocío Zambrano.

SUGGESTED READING

Kramer, Samuel Noah. *The Sumerians: Their History, Culture, and Character*. The University of Chicago Press: Chicago, 1963.

Morley, Jacqueline. *You Wouldn't Want to be a Sumerian Slave!* Franklin Watts: New York, 2007.